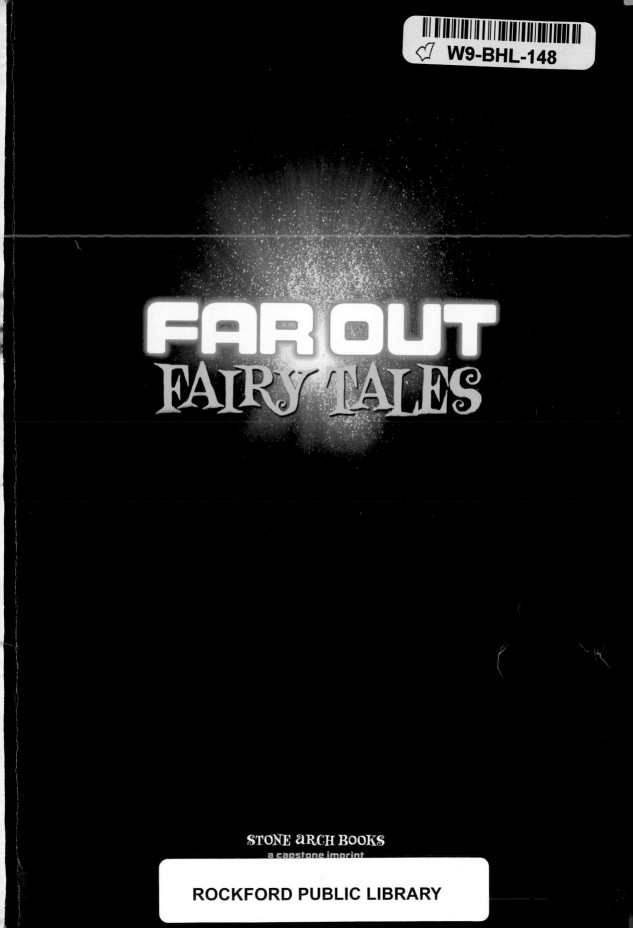

FAR OUT FAIRY TALES

STONE ARCH BOOKS
a capstone imprint

INTRODUCING...

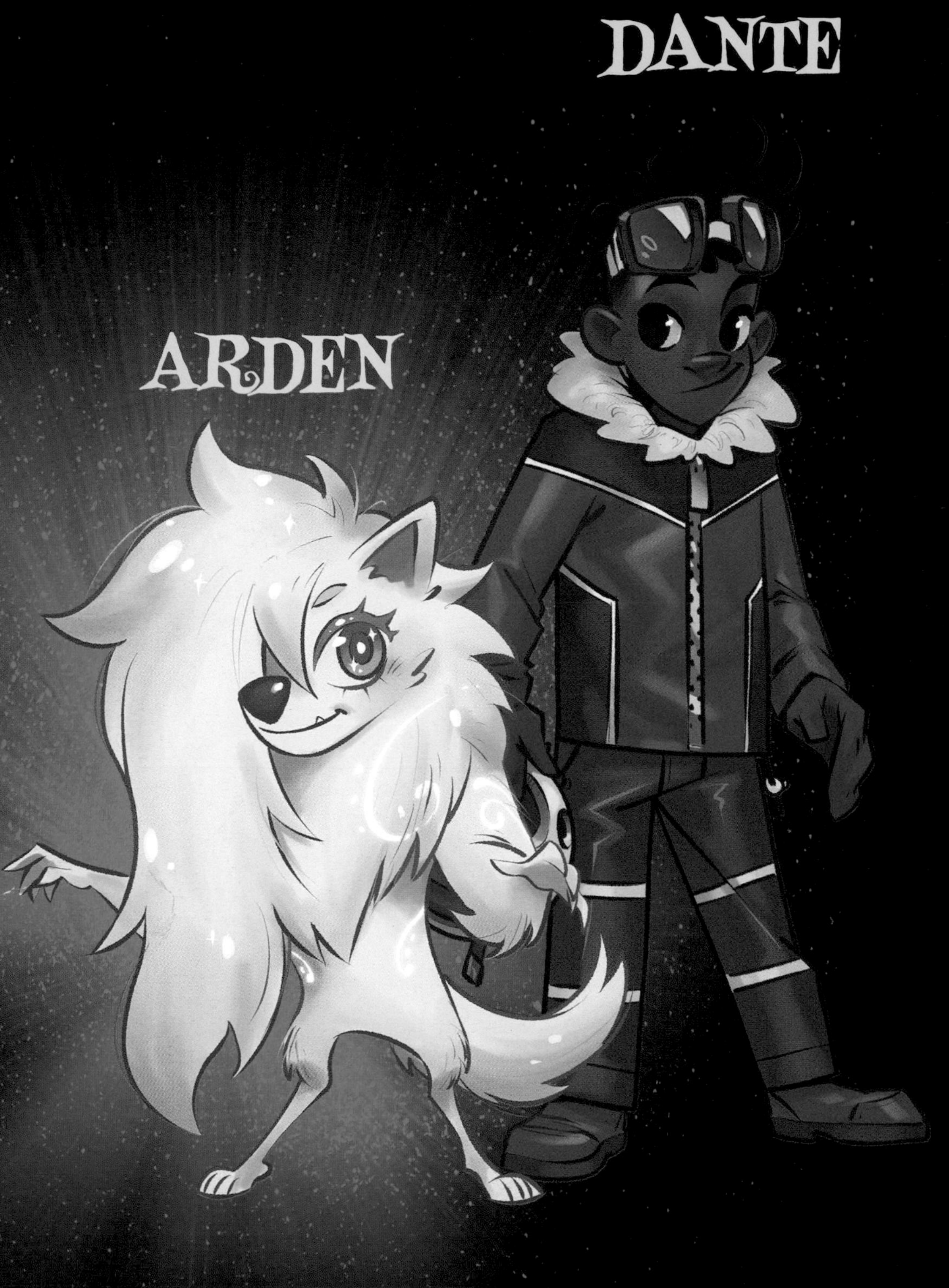
DANTE
ARDEN

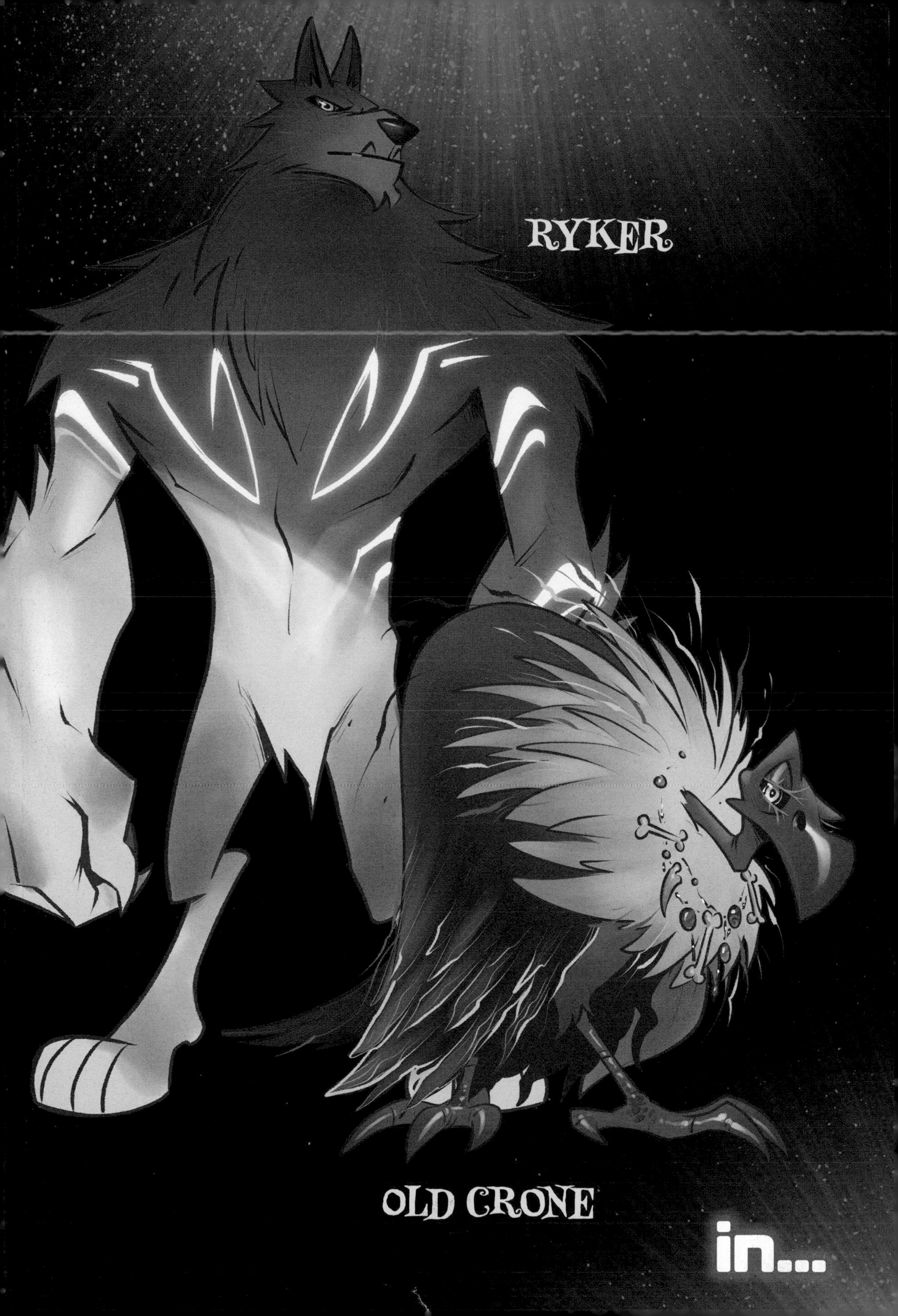
RYKER
OLD CRONE
in...

Far Out Fairy Tales is published by
Stone Arch Books
a Capstone imprint
1710 Roe Crest Drive
North Mankato, Minnesota 56003
www.capstonepub.com

Cataloging-in-Publication Data is available
at the Library of Congress website.
ISBN: 978-1-4965-9684-0 (hardcover)
ISBN: 978-1-4965-9906-3 (paperback)
ISBN: 978-1-4965-9745-8 (eBook PDF)

Summary: In a mountain valley, there
lives a special pack of wolves. When the
moon is full, they become werewolves!
The pack fears the dangers on the far
side of the mountain. But the pack
leader's daughter is curious. She sneaks
over to discover it is a ski resort. She
befriends a young boy there. But will
their friendship survive if he discovers her
dark secret? And what will her pack think
of her dangerous friendship?

Designed by Hilary Wacholz
Edited by Mandy Robbins
Lettered by Jaymes Reed

Printed and bound in the USA.
PA117

FAR OUT FAIRY TALES

THE LITTLE WEREWOLF

A GRAPHIC NOVEL

BY STEPHANIE PETERS

ILLUSTRATED BY OMAR LOZANO

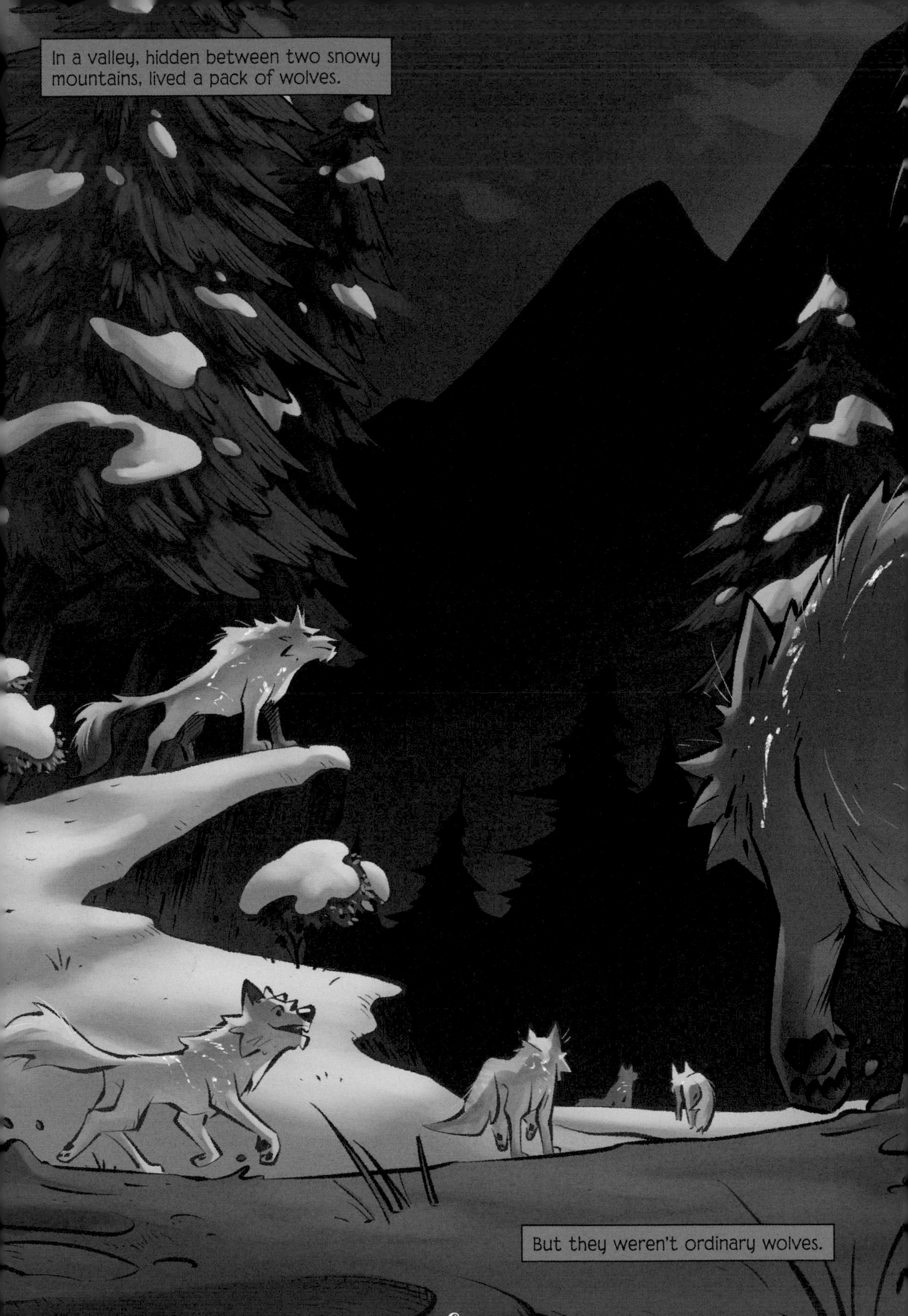
In a valley, hidden between two snowy mountains, lived a pack of wolves.
But they weren't ordinary wolves.

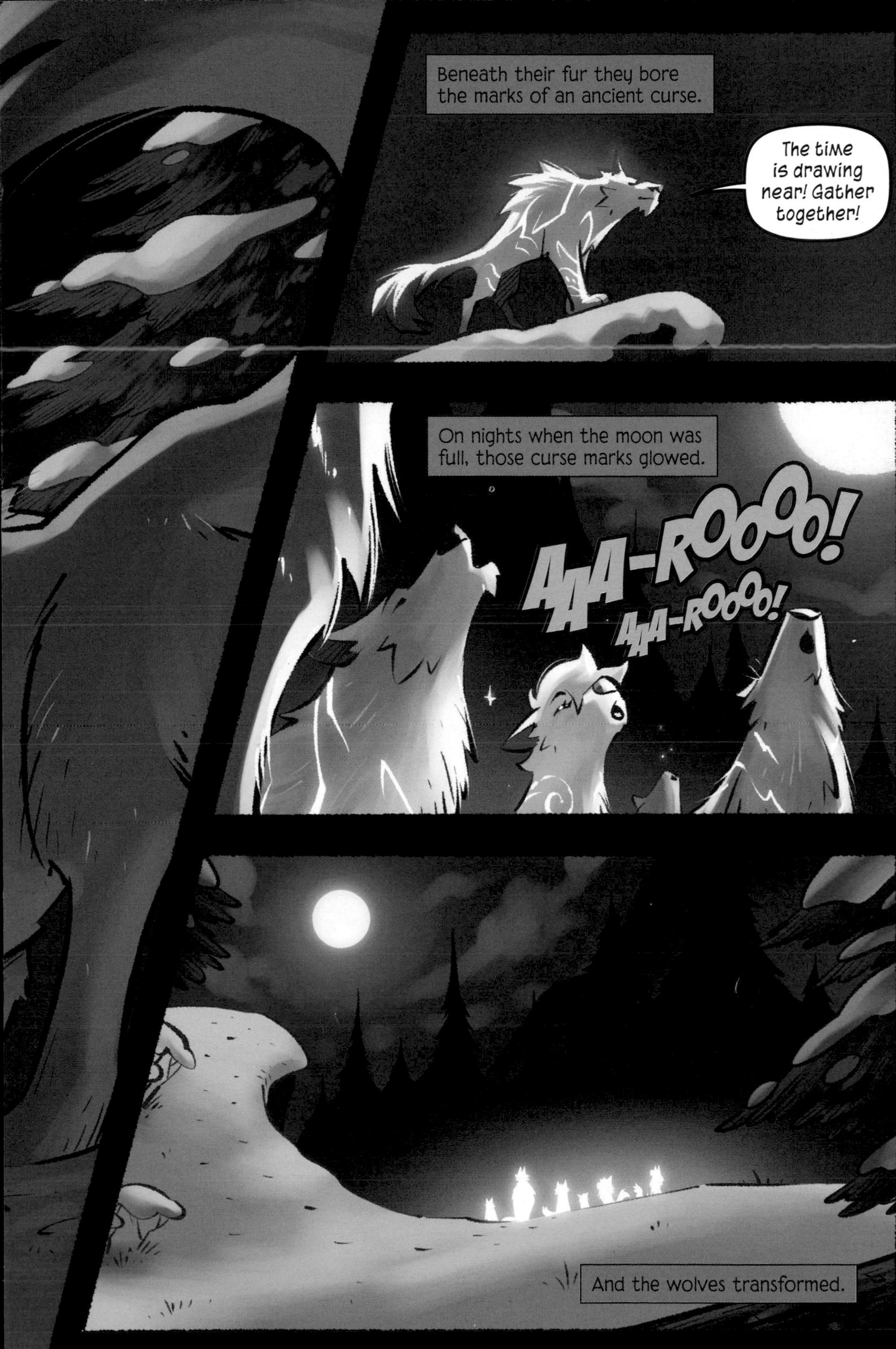

Beneath their fur they bore the marks of an ancient curse.
The time is drawing near! Gather together!
On nights when the moon was full, those curse marks glowed.
AAA-ROOOOO!
AAA-ROOOO!
And the wolves transformed.

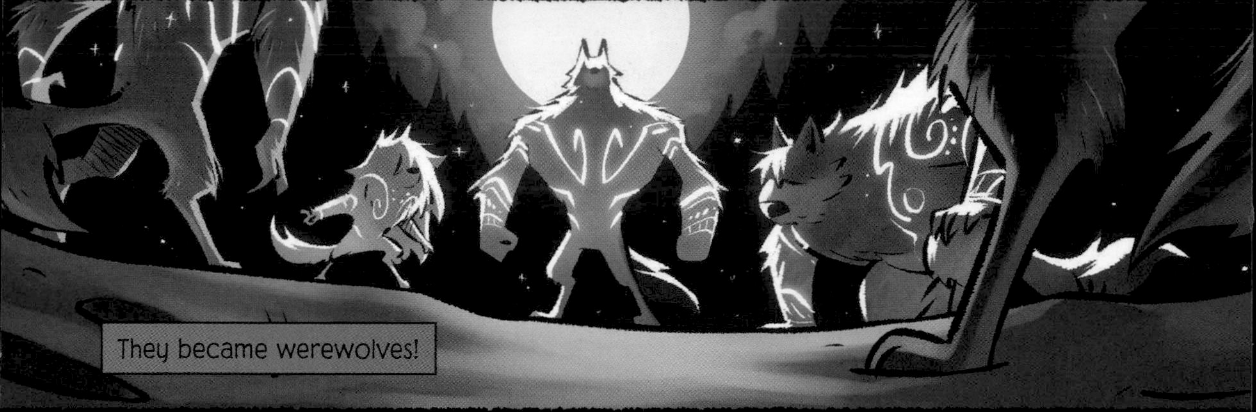
They became werewolves!

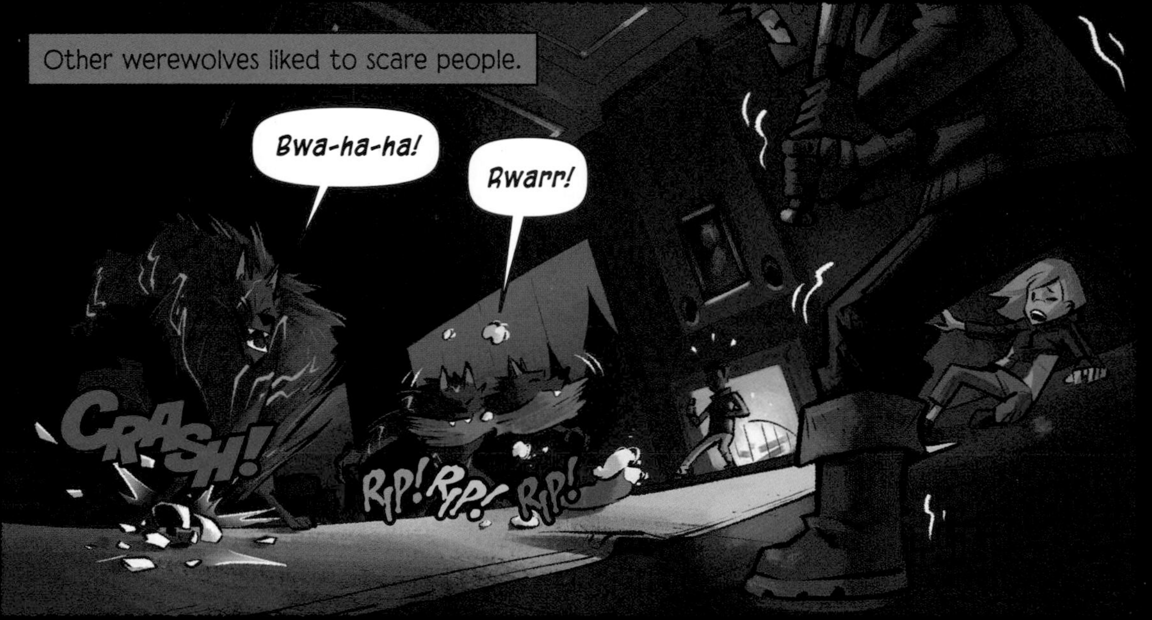
Other werewolves liked to scare people.
Bwa-ha-ha!
Rwarr!
CRASH!
RIP! RIP! RIP!

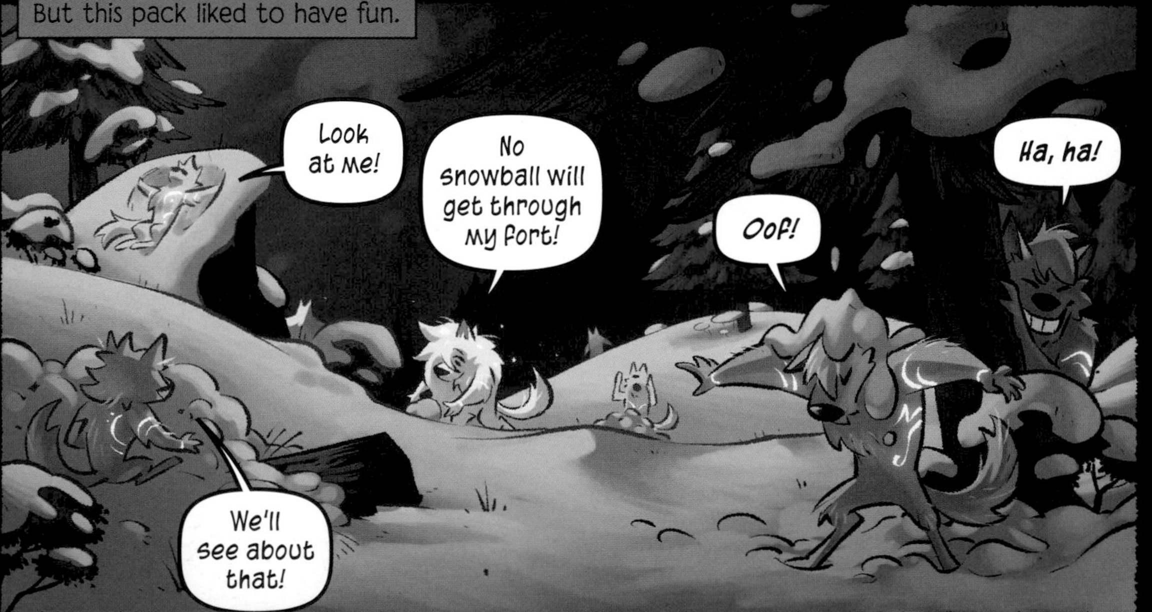
But this pack liked to have fun.
Look at me!
No snowball will get through my fort!
Oof!
Ha, ha!
We'll see about that!

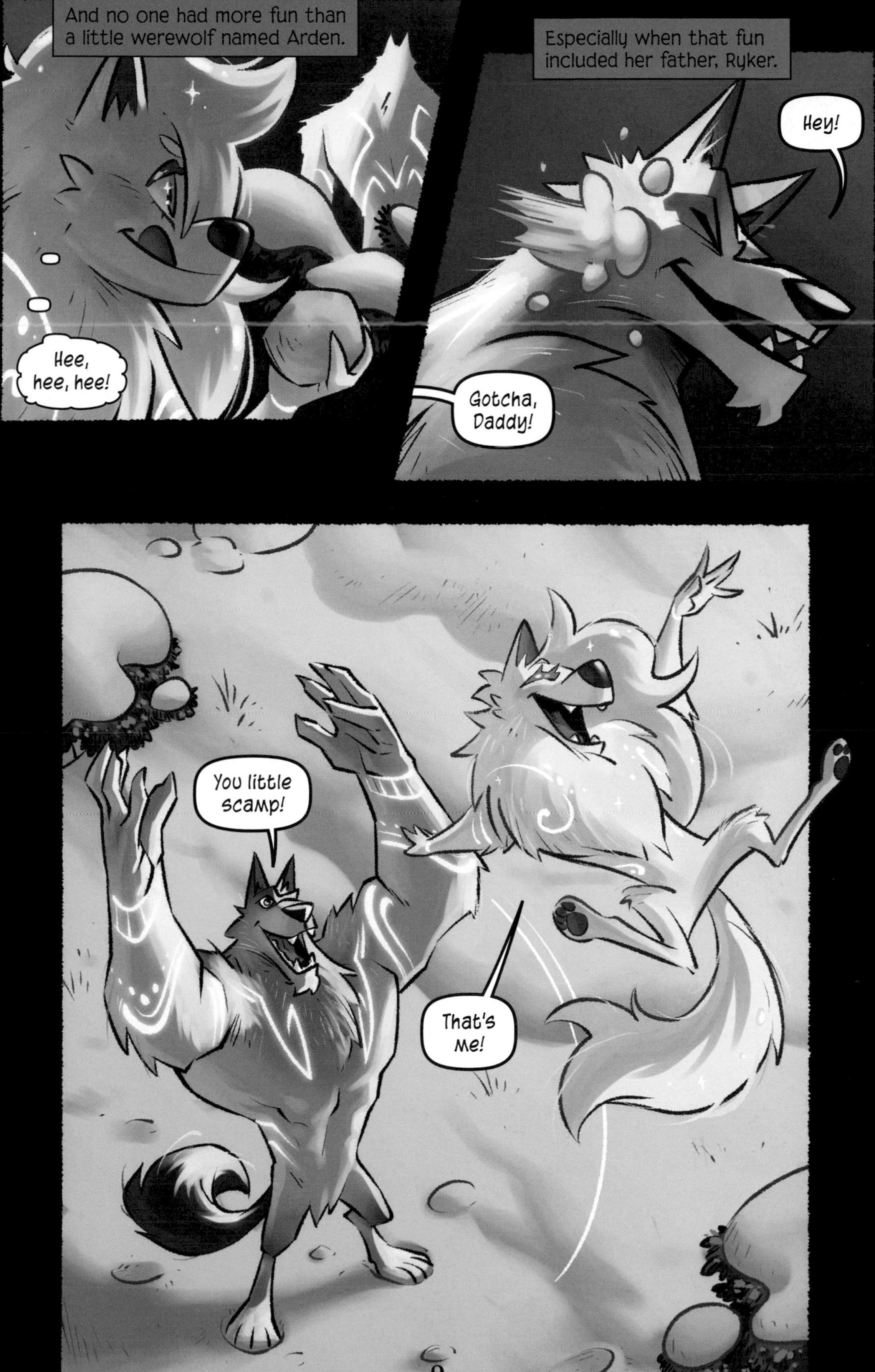

And no one had more fun than a little werewolf named Arden.
Hee, hee, hee!
Especially when that fun included her father, Ryker.
Hey!
Gotcha, Daddy!
You little scamp!
That's me!

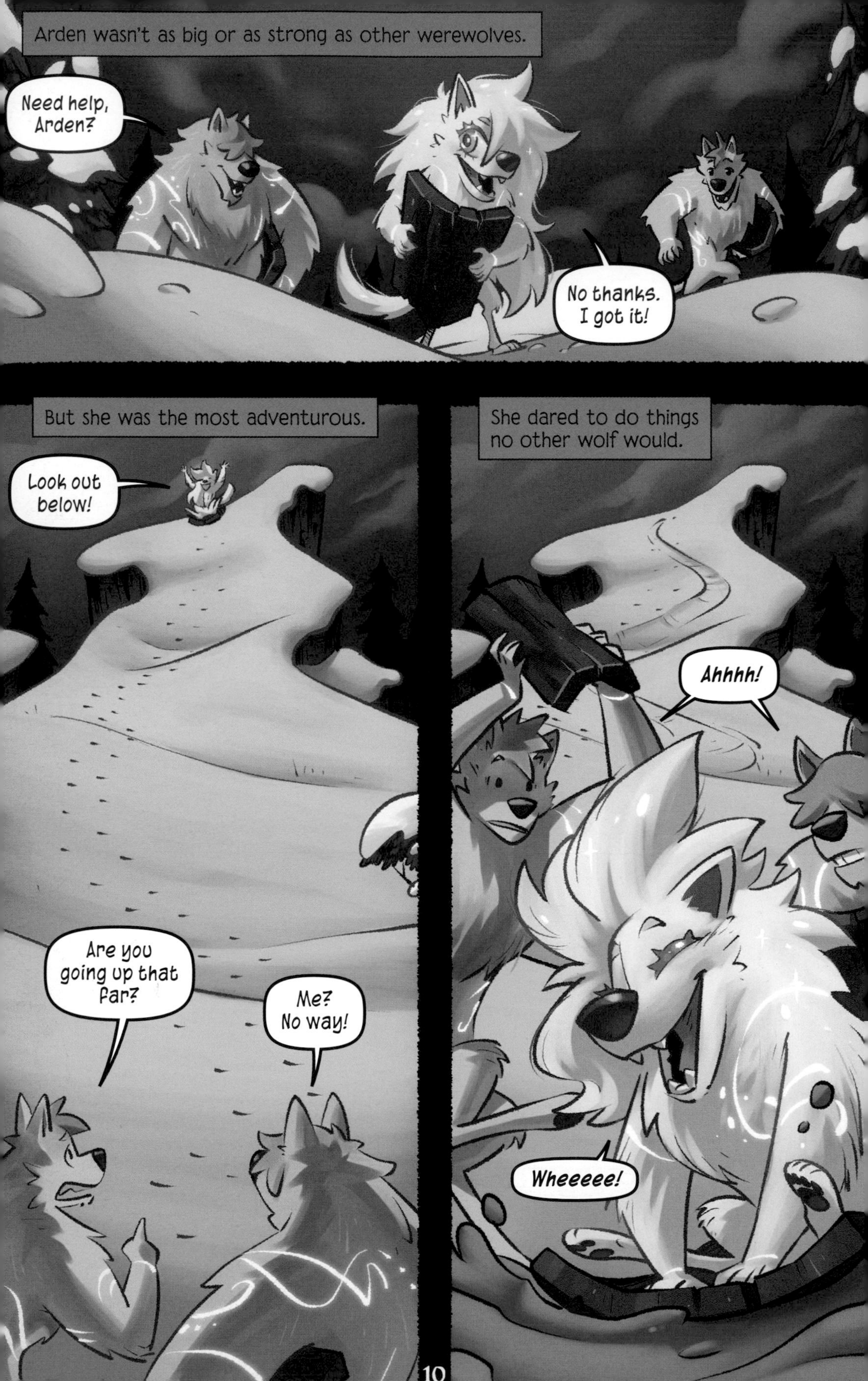

Arden wasn't as big or as strong as other werewolves.
Need help, Arden?
No thanks. I got it!
But she was the most adventurous.
Look out below!
Are you going up that far?
Me? No way!
She dared to do things no other wolf would.
Ahhhh!
Wheeeee!

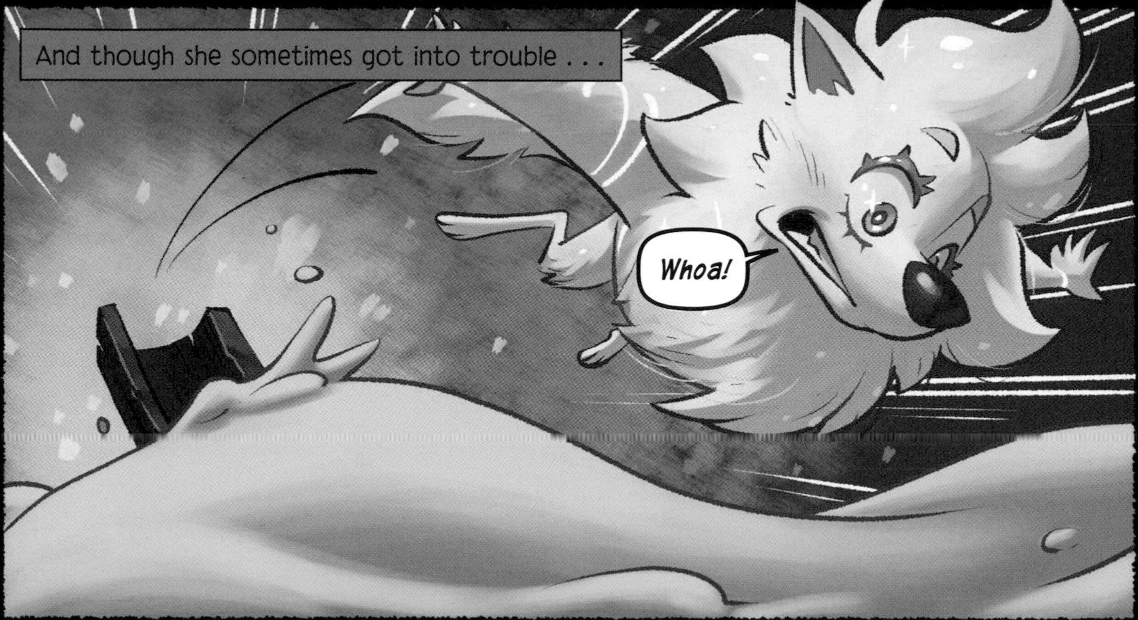
And though she sometimes got into trouble . . .
Whoa!

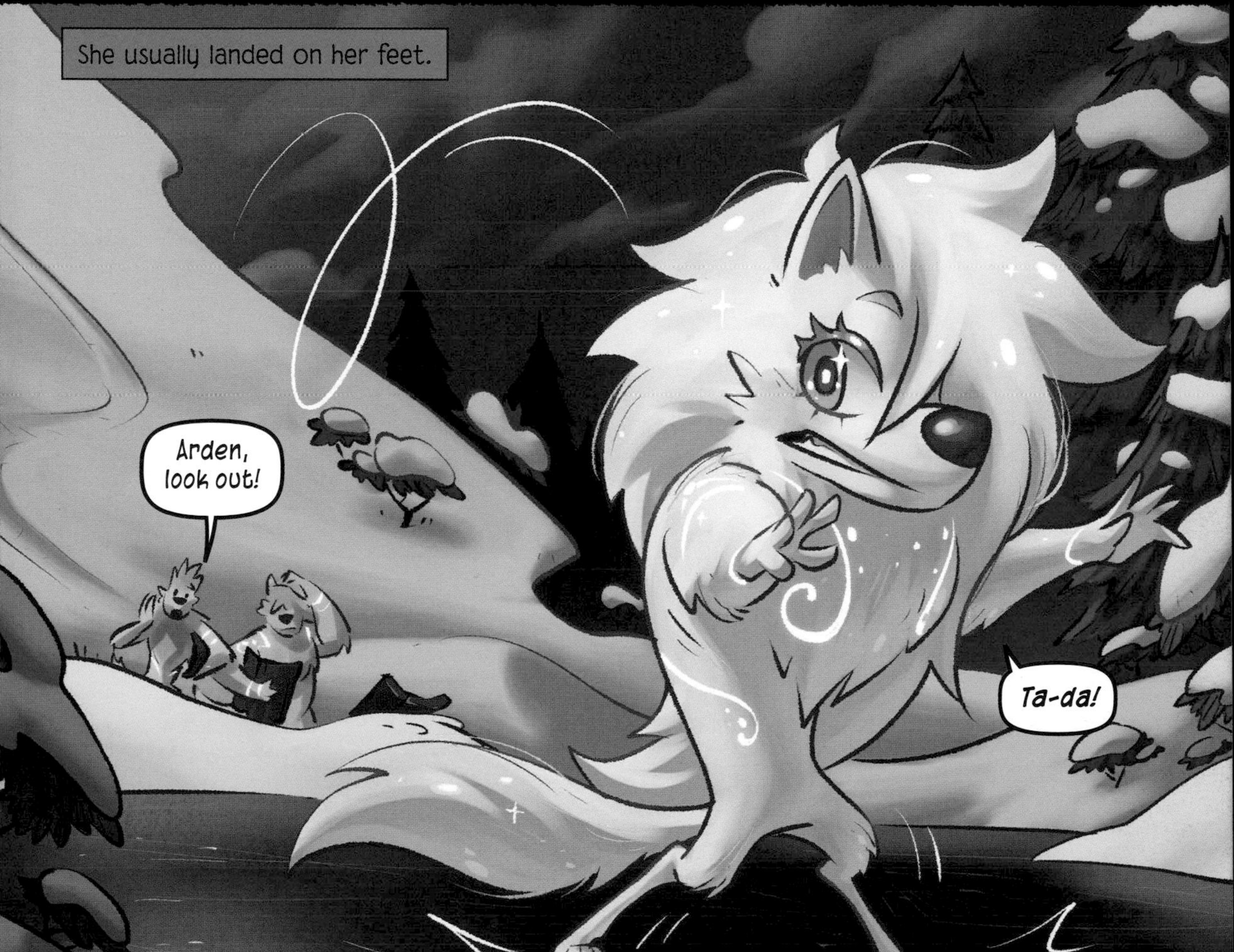
She usually landed on her feet.
Arden, look out!
Ta-da!

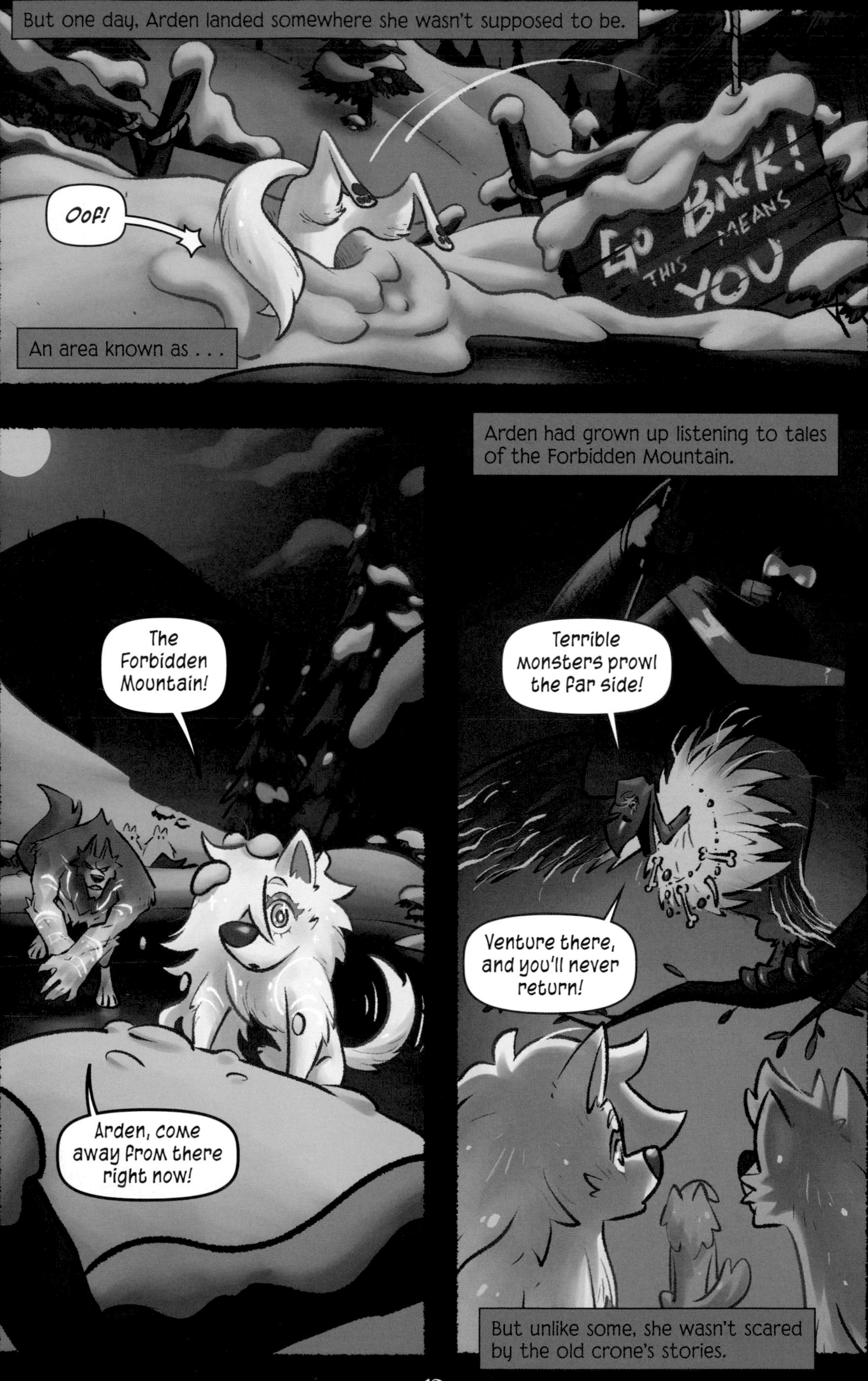
But one day, Arden landed somewhere she wasn't supposed to be.
Oof!
GO BACK! THIS MEANS YOU
An area known as . . .
The Forbidden Mountain!
Arden, come away from there right now!
Arden had grown up listening to tales of the Forbidden Mountain.
Terrible monsters prowl the far side!
Venture there, and you'll never return!
But unlike some, she wasn't scared by the old crone's stories.

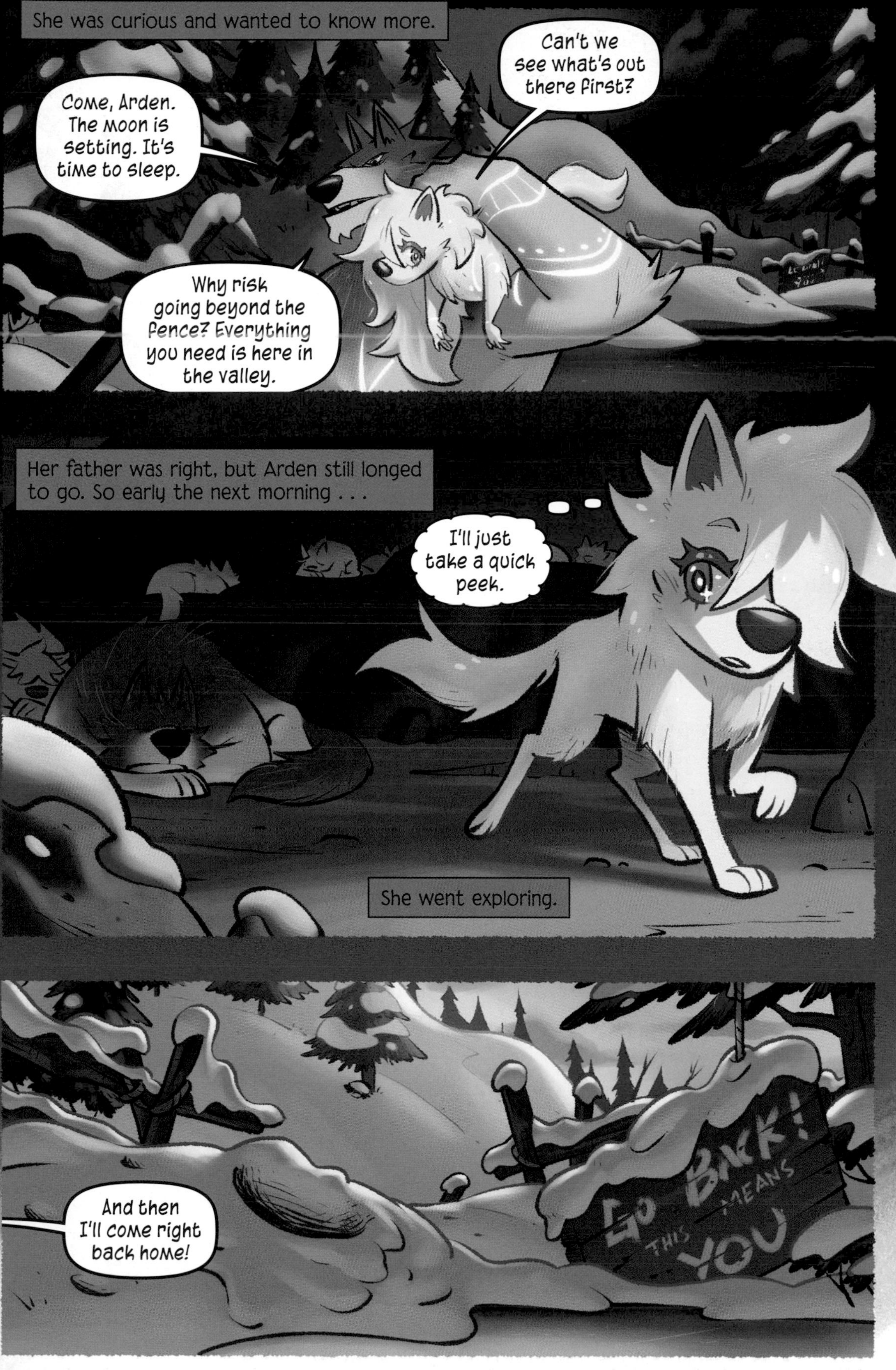

She was curious and wanted to know more.
Come, Arden. The moon is setting. It's time to sleep.
Can't we see what's out there first?
Why risk going beyond the fence? Everything you need is here in the valley.
Her father was right, but Arden still longed to go. So early the next morning . . .
I'll just take a quick peek.
She went exploring.
And then I'll come right back home!
GO BACK! THIS MEANS YOU

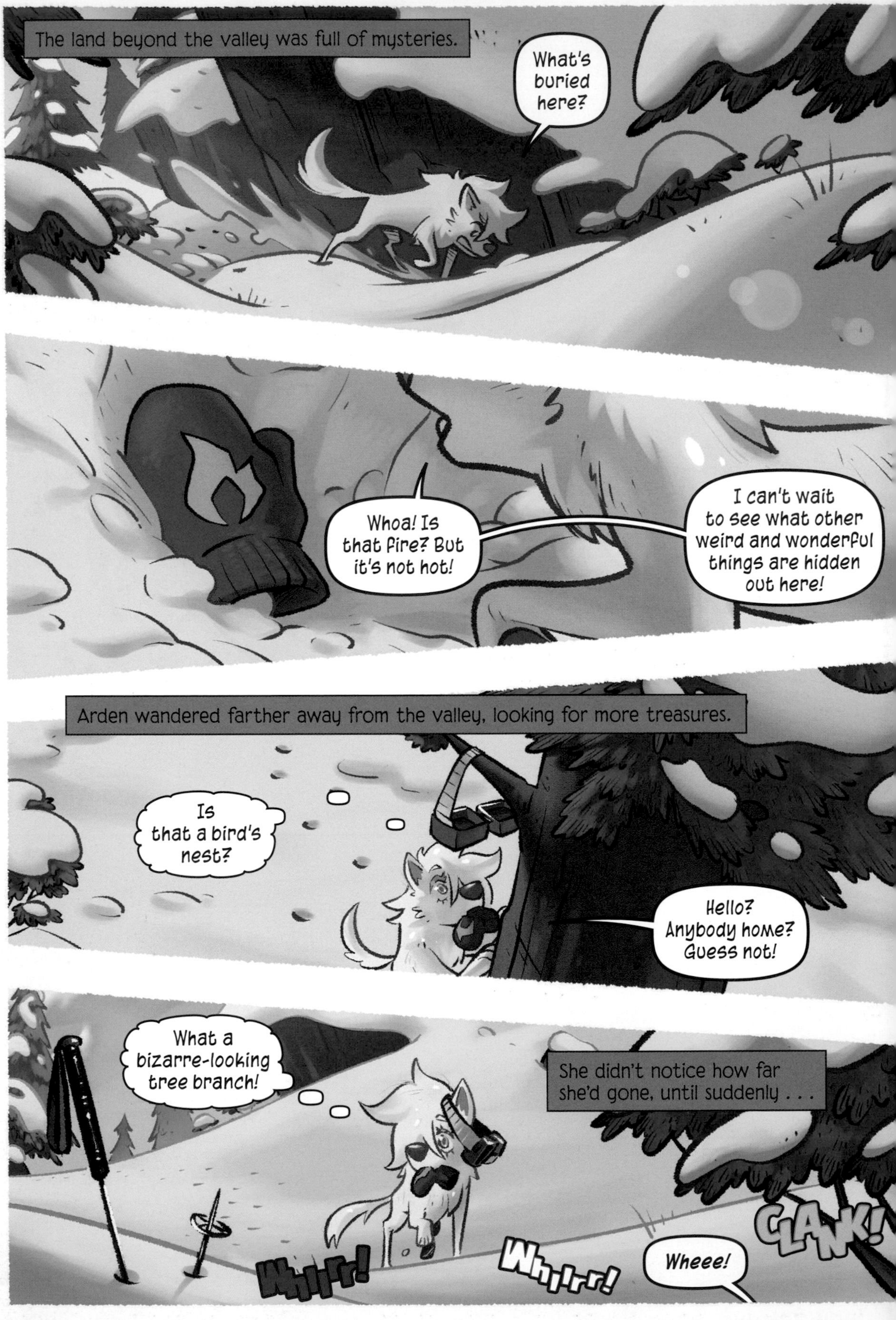
The land beyond the valley was full of mysteries.
What's buried here?
Whoa! Is that fire? But it's not hot!
I can't wait to see what other weird and wonderful things are hidden out here!
Arden wandered farther away from the valley, looking for more treasures.
Is that a bird's nest?
Hello? Anybody home? Guess not!
What a bizarre-looking tree branch!
She didn't notice how far she'd gone, until suddenly . . .
Whirrr!
Whirrr!
Wheee!
CLANK!

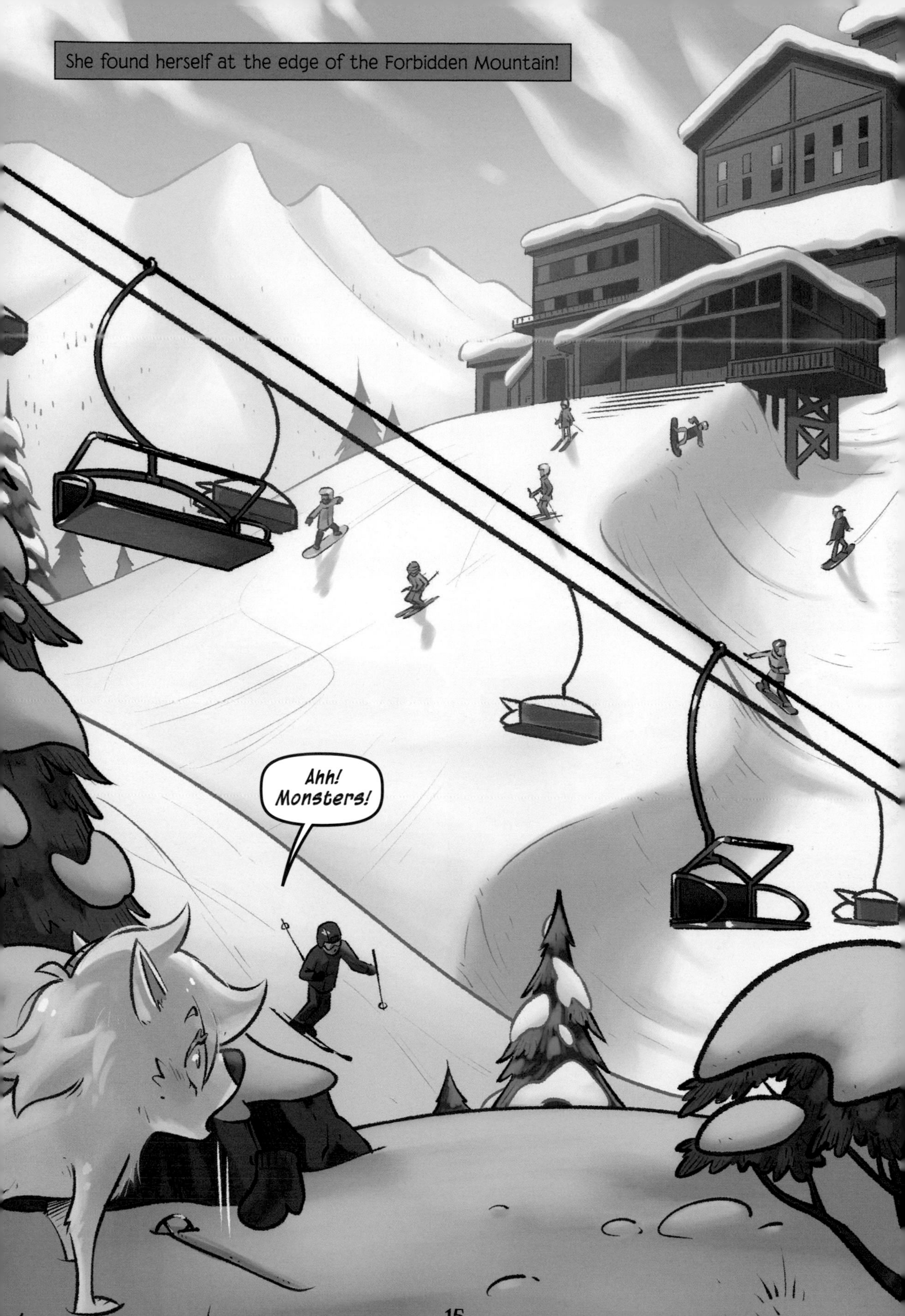
She found herself at the edge of the Forbidden Mountain!
Ahh! Monsters!

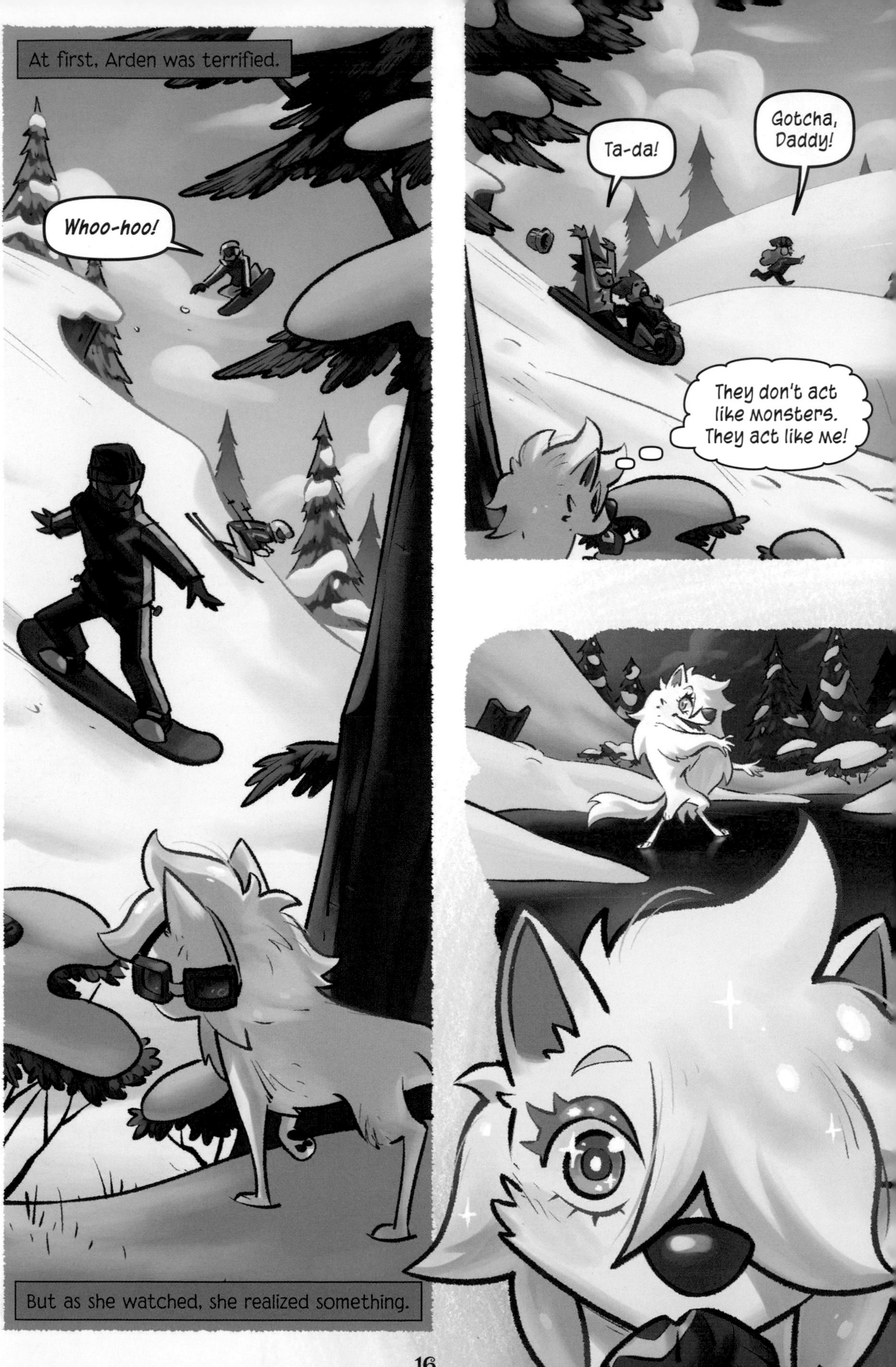
At first, Arden was terrified.
Whoo-hoo!
But as she watched, she realized something.
Ta-da!
Gotcha, Daddy!
They don't act like monsters. They act like me!

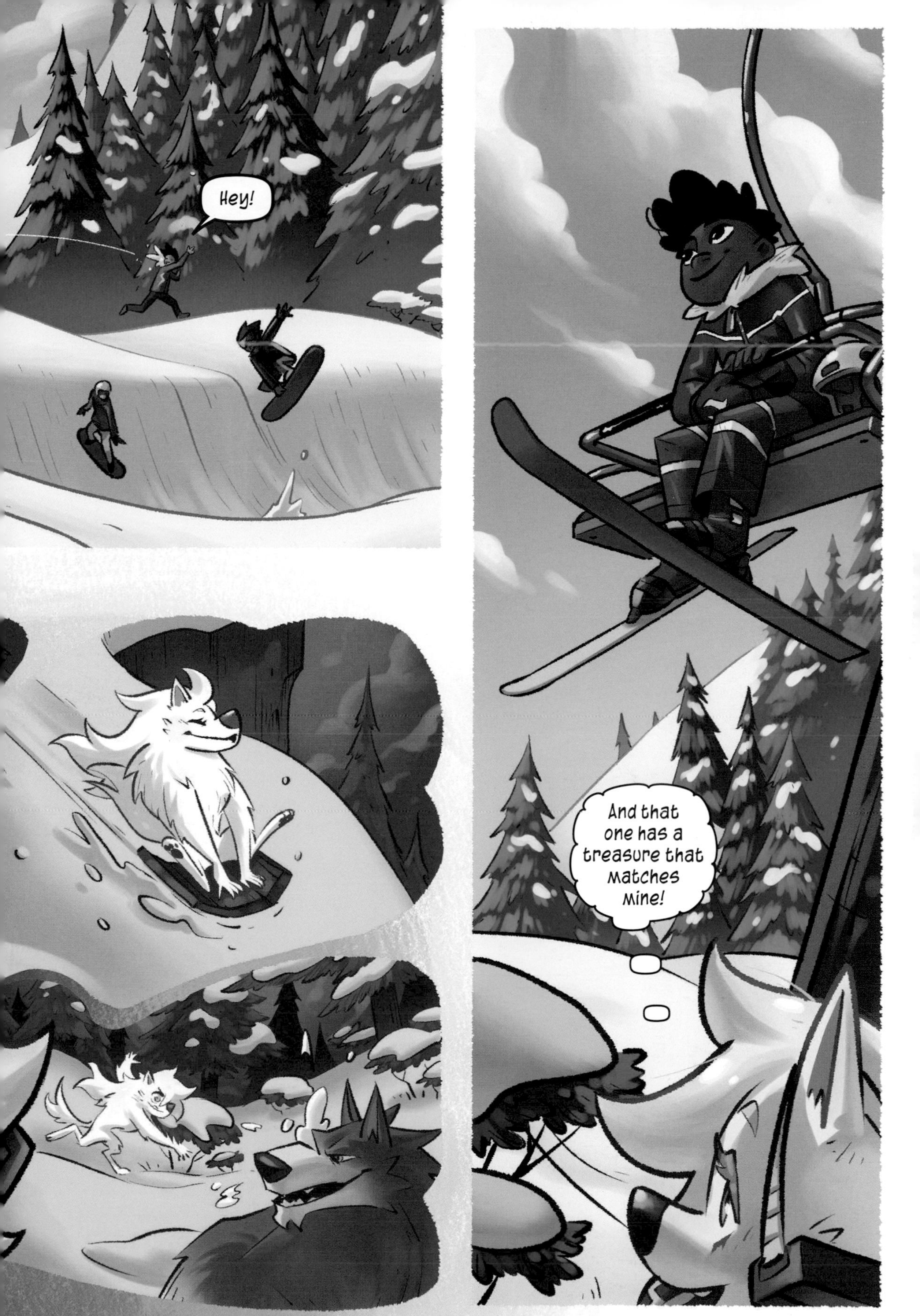
Hey!
And that one has a treasure that matches mine!

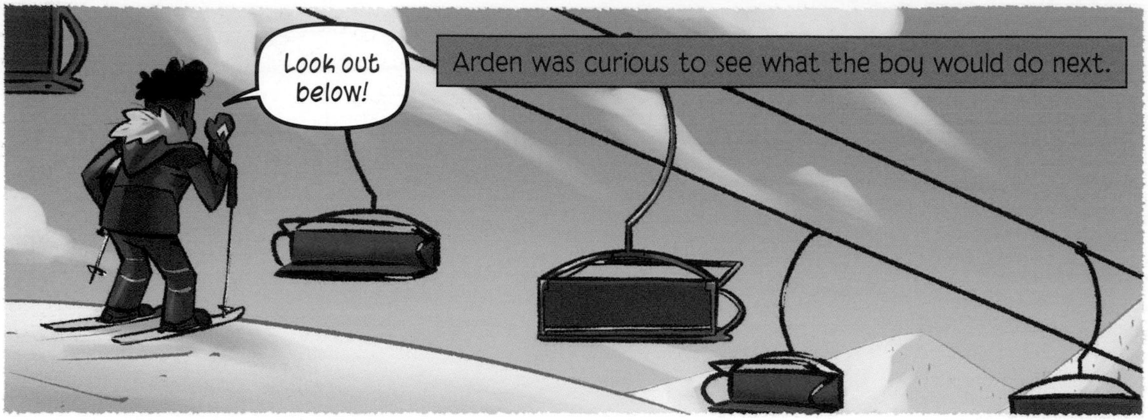
Look out below!
Arden was curious to see what the boy would do next.

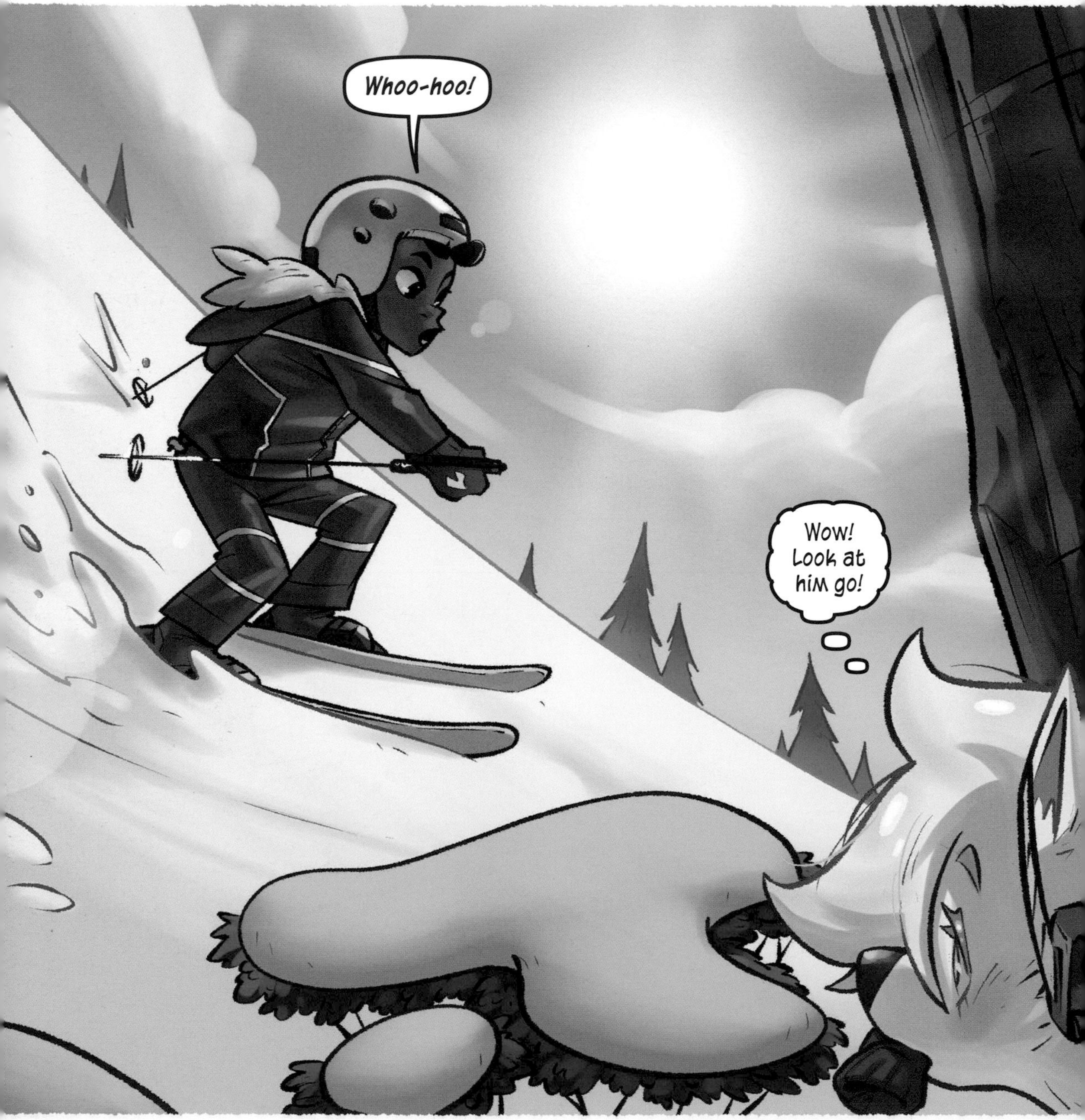
Whoo-hoo!
Wow! Look at him go!

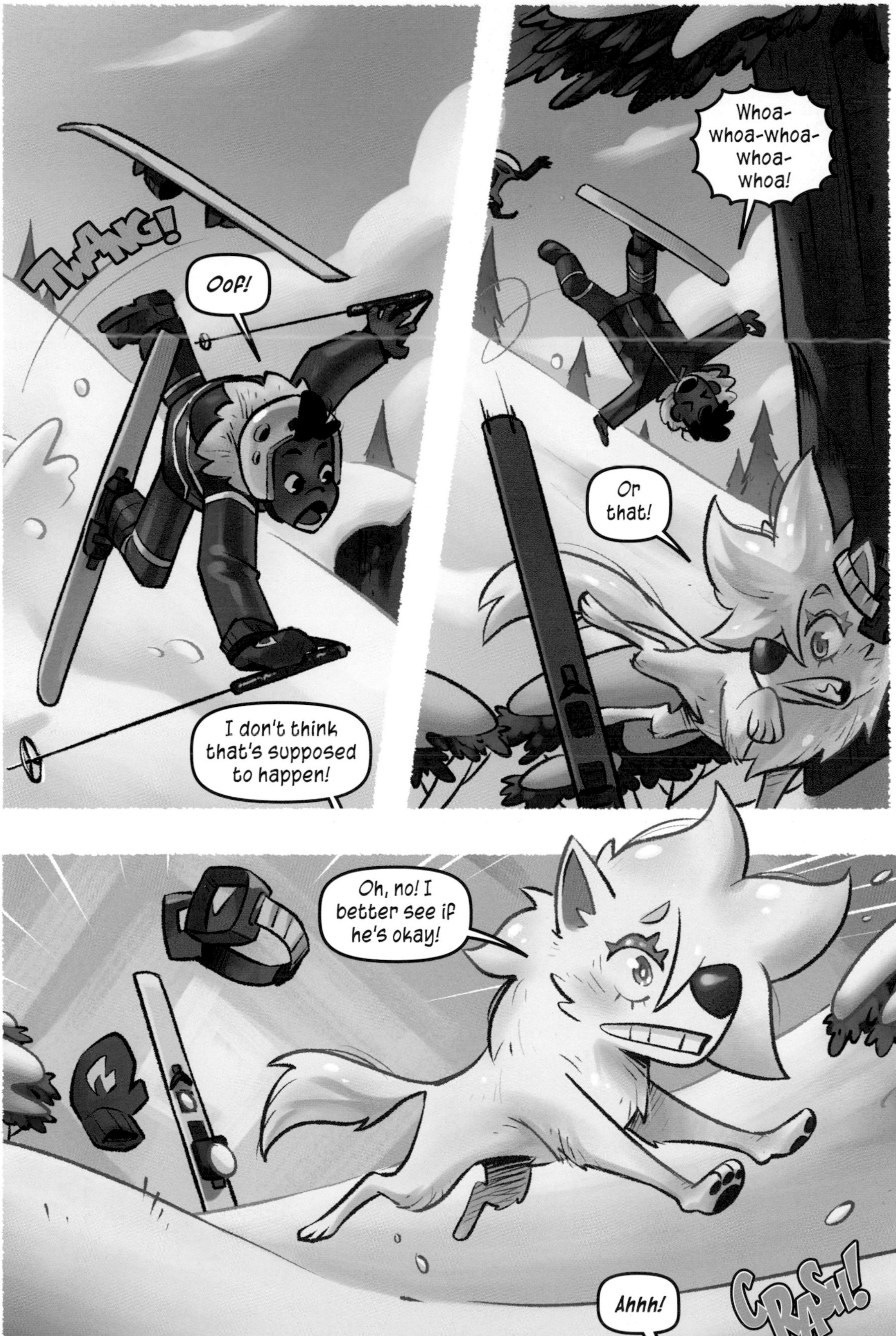
TWANG!
Oof!
I don't think that's supposed to happen!
Whoa-whoa-whoa-whoa-whoa!
Or that!
Oh, no! I better see if he's okay!
Ahhh!
CRASH!

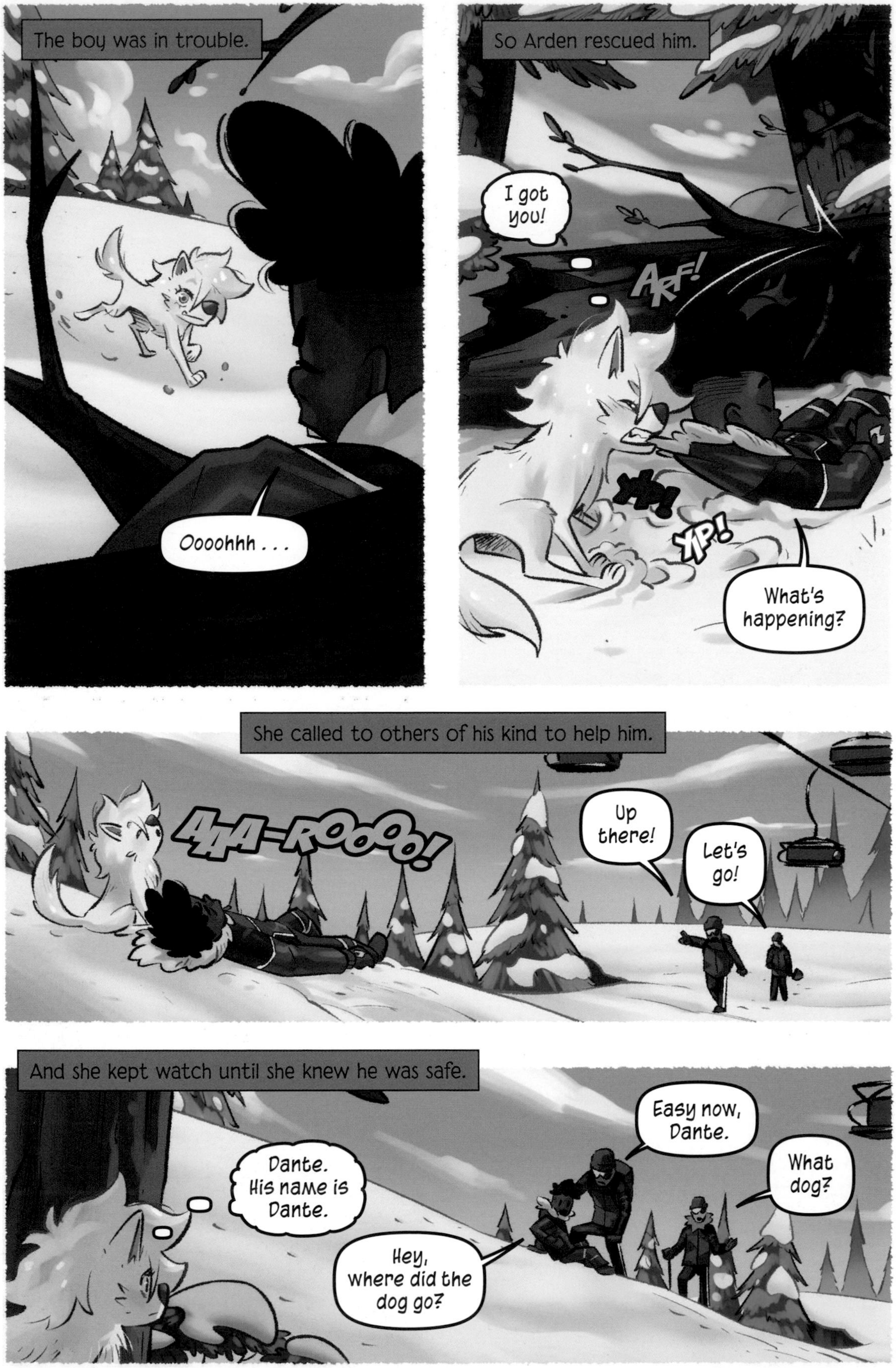
The boy was in trouble.
Oooohhh . . .
So Arden rescued him.
I got you!
ARF!
YIP!
YIP!
What's happening?
She called to others of his kind to help him.
AAA-ROOOOO!
Up there!
Let's go!
And she kept watch until she knew he was safe.
Easy now, Dante.
What dog?
Dante. His name is Dante.
Hey, where did the dog go?

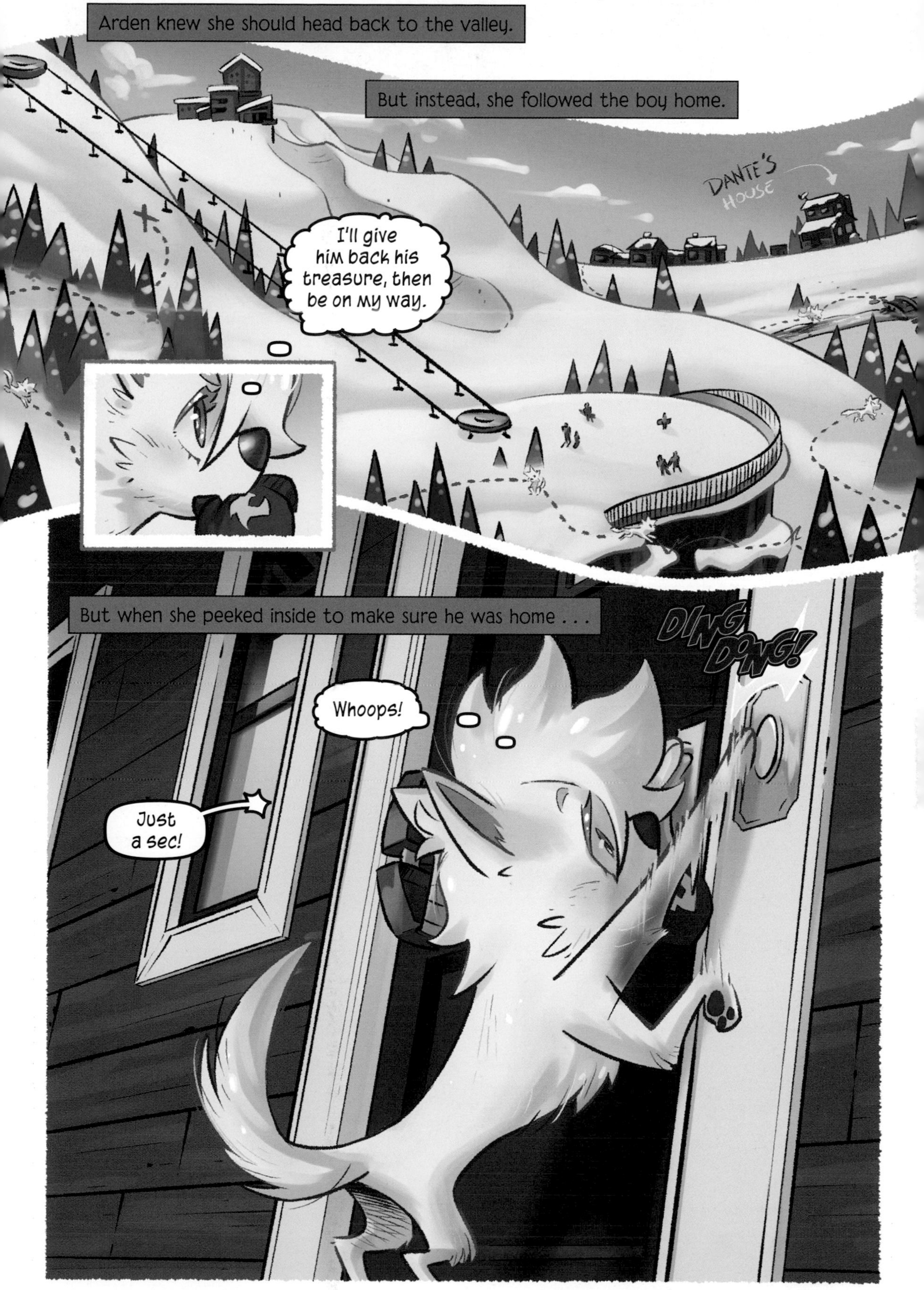

Arden knew she should head back to the valley.
But instead, she followed the boy home.
DANTE'S HOUSE
I'll give him back his treasure, then be on my way.
But when she peeked inside to make sure he was home . . .
DING DONG!
Whoops!
Just a sec!

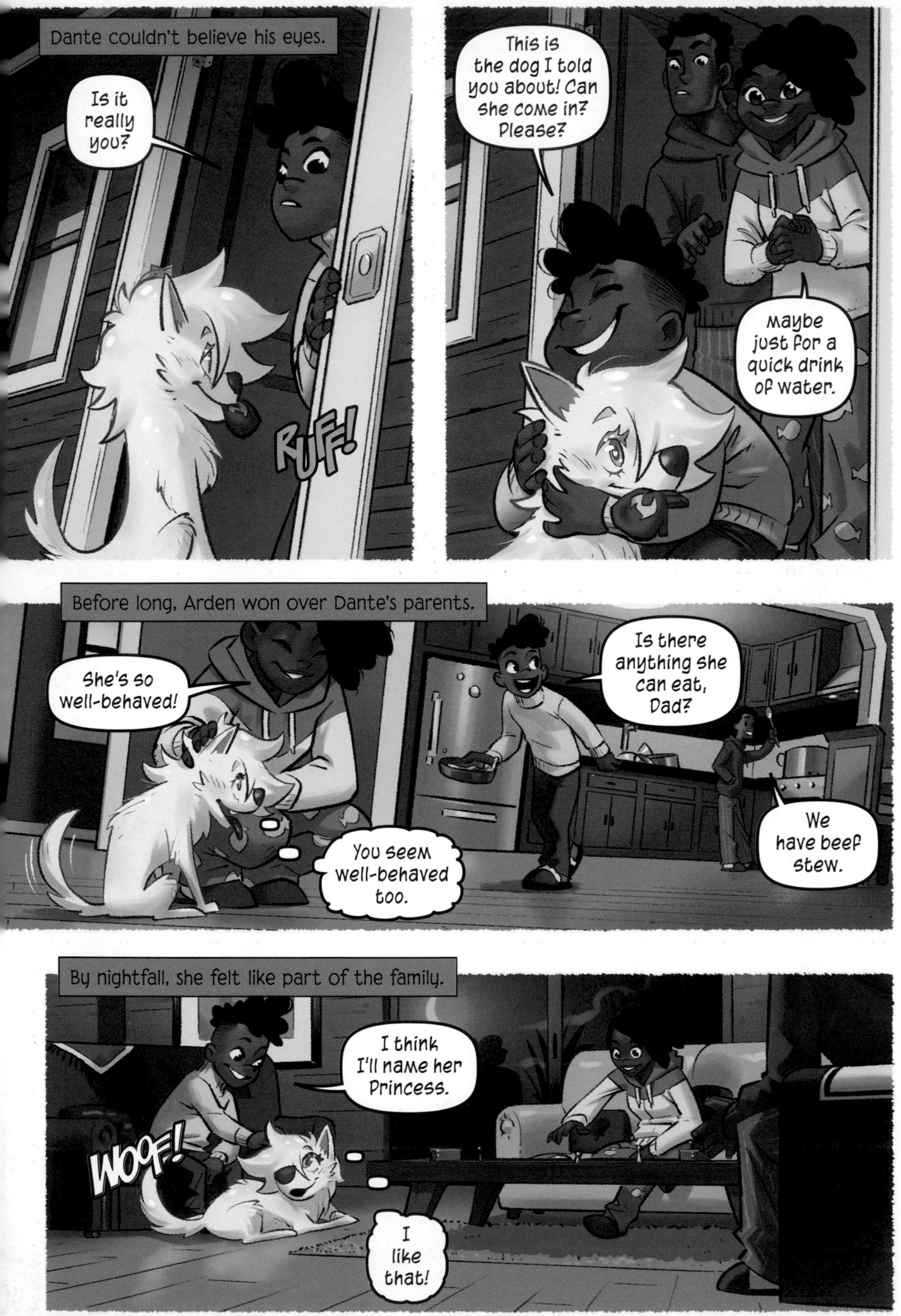
Dante couldn't believe his eyes.
Is it really you?
RUFF!
This is the dog I told you about! Can she come in? Please?
Maybe just for a quick drink of water.
Before long, Arden won over Dante's parents.
She's so well-behaved!
You seem well-behaved too.
Is there anything she can eat, Dad?
We have beef stew.
By nightfall, she felt like part of the family.
I think I'll name her Princess.
WOOF!
I like that!

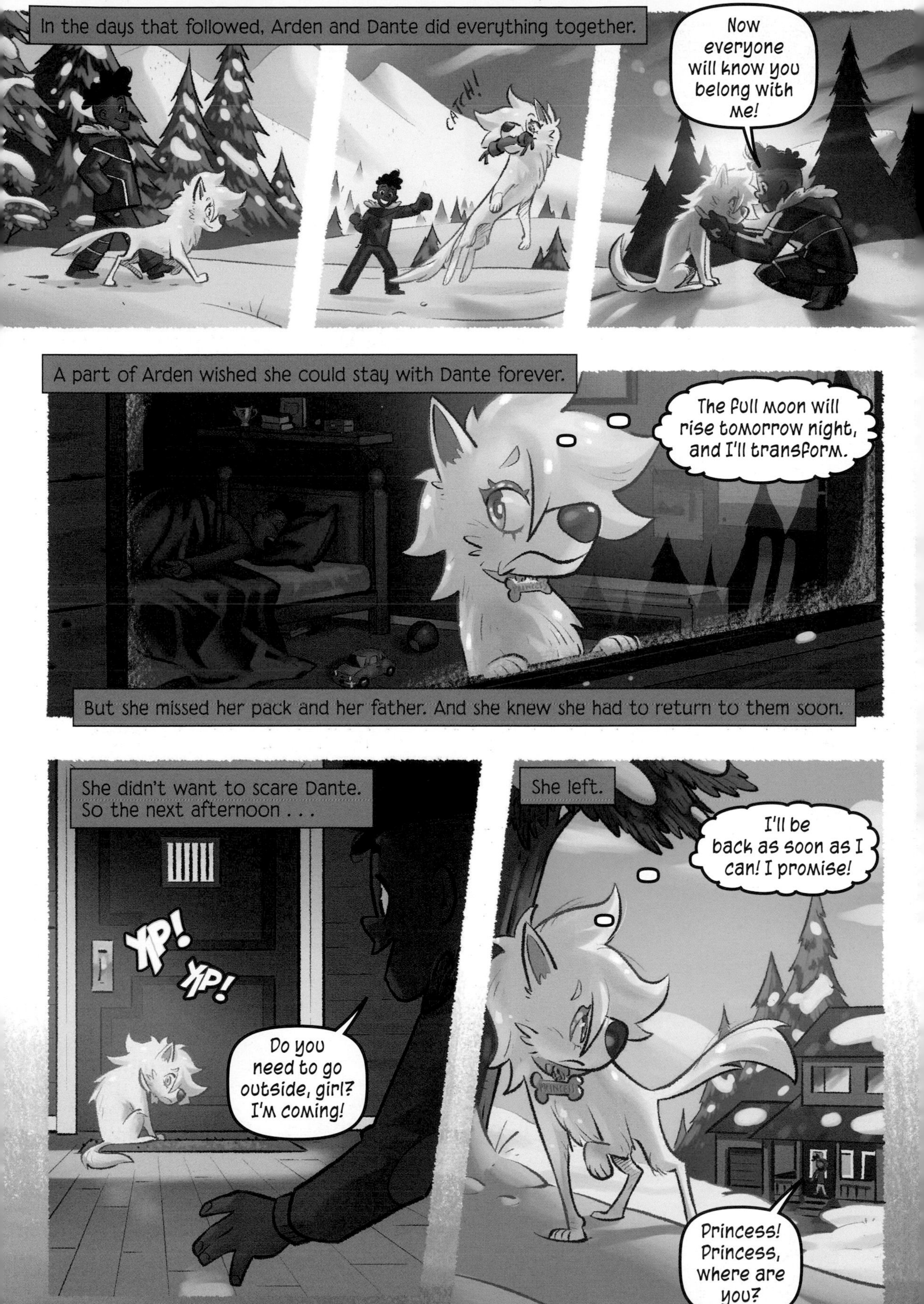
In the days that followed, Arden and Dante did everything together.
CATCH!
Now everyone will know you belong with me!
A part of Arden wished she could stay with Dante forever.
The full moon will rise tomorrow night, and I'll transform.
But she missed her pack and her father. And she knew she had to return to them soon.
She didn't want to scare Dante. So the next afternoon . . .
YIP! YIP!
Do you need to go outside, girl? I'm coming!
She left.
I'll be back as soon as I can! I promise!
Princess! Princess, where are you?

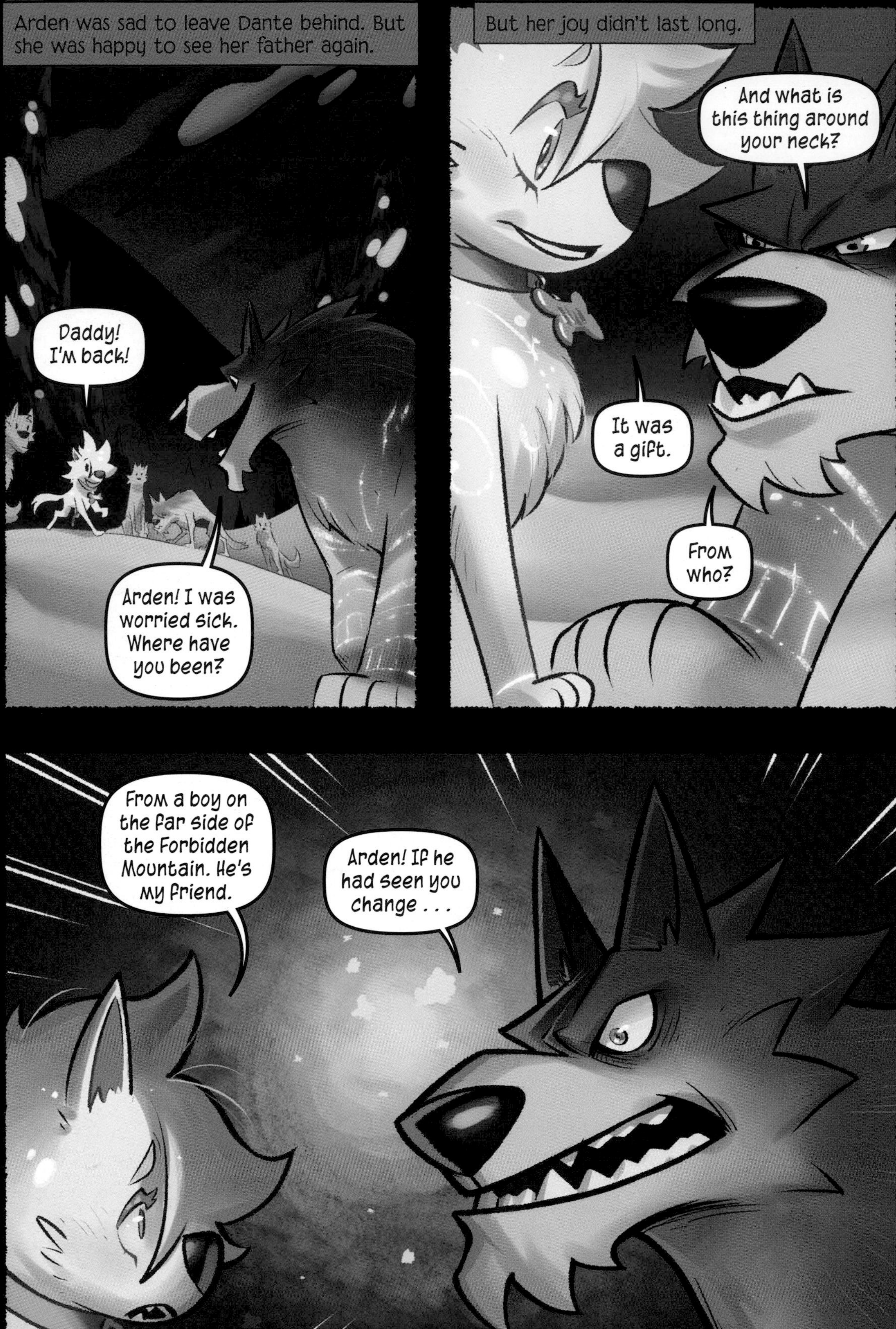
Arden was sad to leave Dante behind. But she was happy to see her father again.
Daddy! I'm back!
Arden! I was worried sick. Where have you been?
But her joy didn't last long.
And what is this thing around your neck?
It was a gift.
From who?
From a boy on the far side of the Forbidden Mountain. He's my friend.
Arden! If he had seen you change . . .

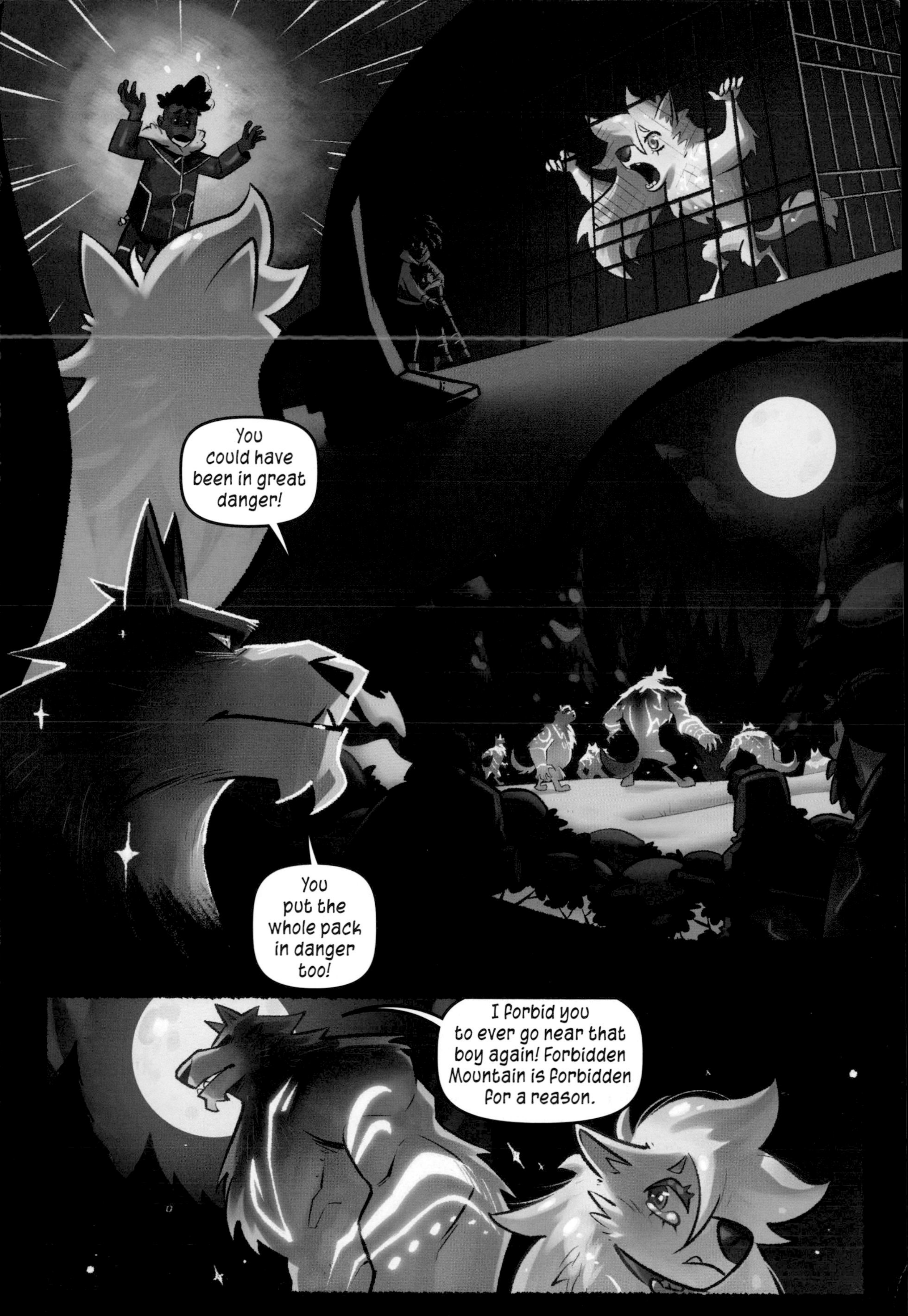
You could have been in great danger!
You put the whole pack in danger too!
I forbid you to ever go near that boy again! Forbidden Mountain is forbidden for a reason.

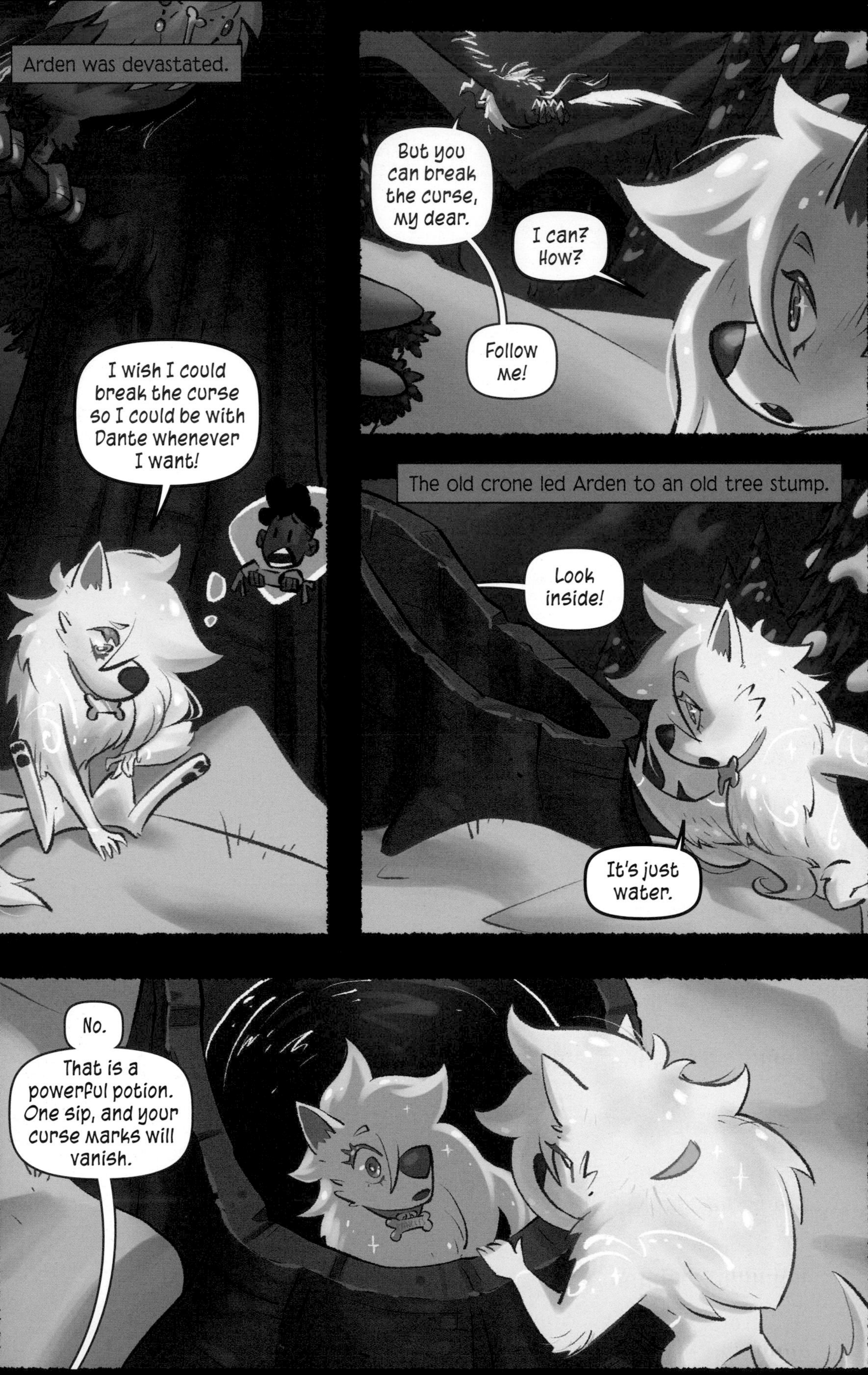
Arden was devastated.
I wish I could break the curse so I could be with Dante whenever I want!
But you can break the curse, my dear.
I can? How?
Follow me!
The old crone led Arden to an old tree stump.
Look inside!
It's just water.
No.
That is a powerful potion. One sip, and your curse marks will vanish.

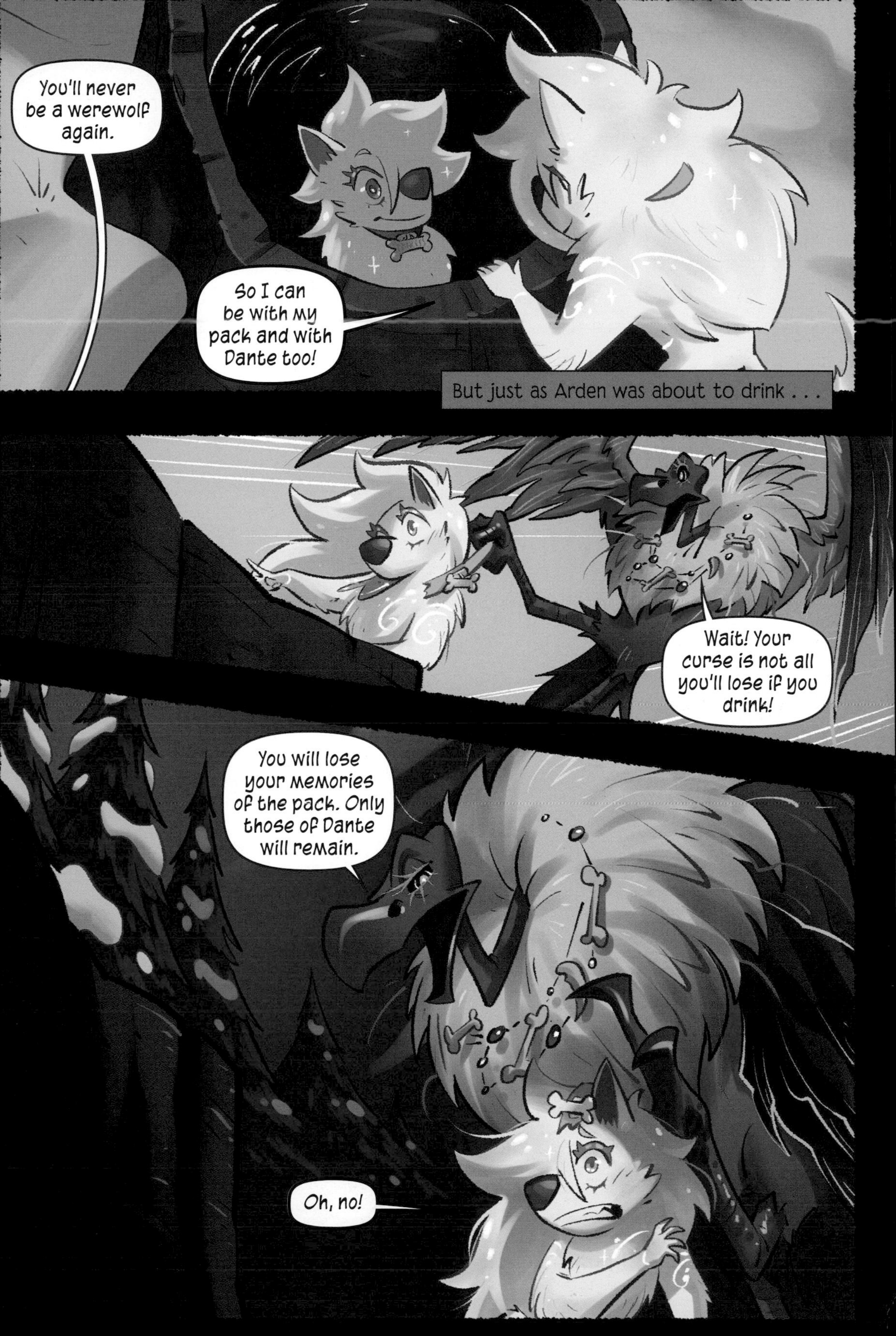
You'll never be a werewolf again.
So I can be with my pack and with Dante too!
But just as Arden was about to drink . . .
Wait! Your curse is not all you'll lose if you drink!
You will lose your memories of the pack. Only those of Dante will remain.
Oh, no!

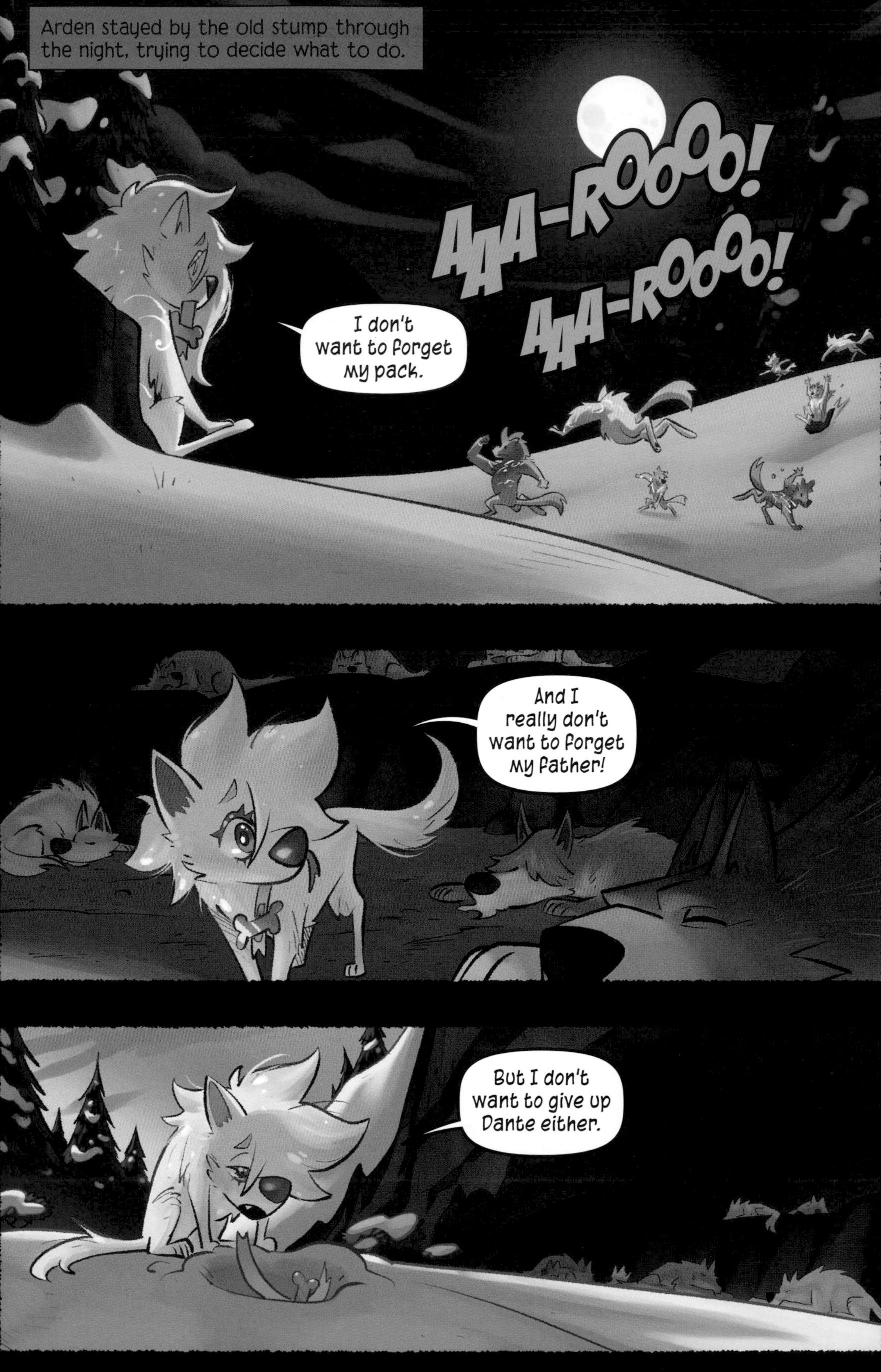
Arden stayed by the old stump through the night, trying to decide what to do.
AAA-ROOOO!
AAA-ROOOO!
I don't want to forget my pack.
And I really don't want to forget my father!
But I don't want to give up Dante either.

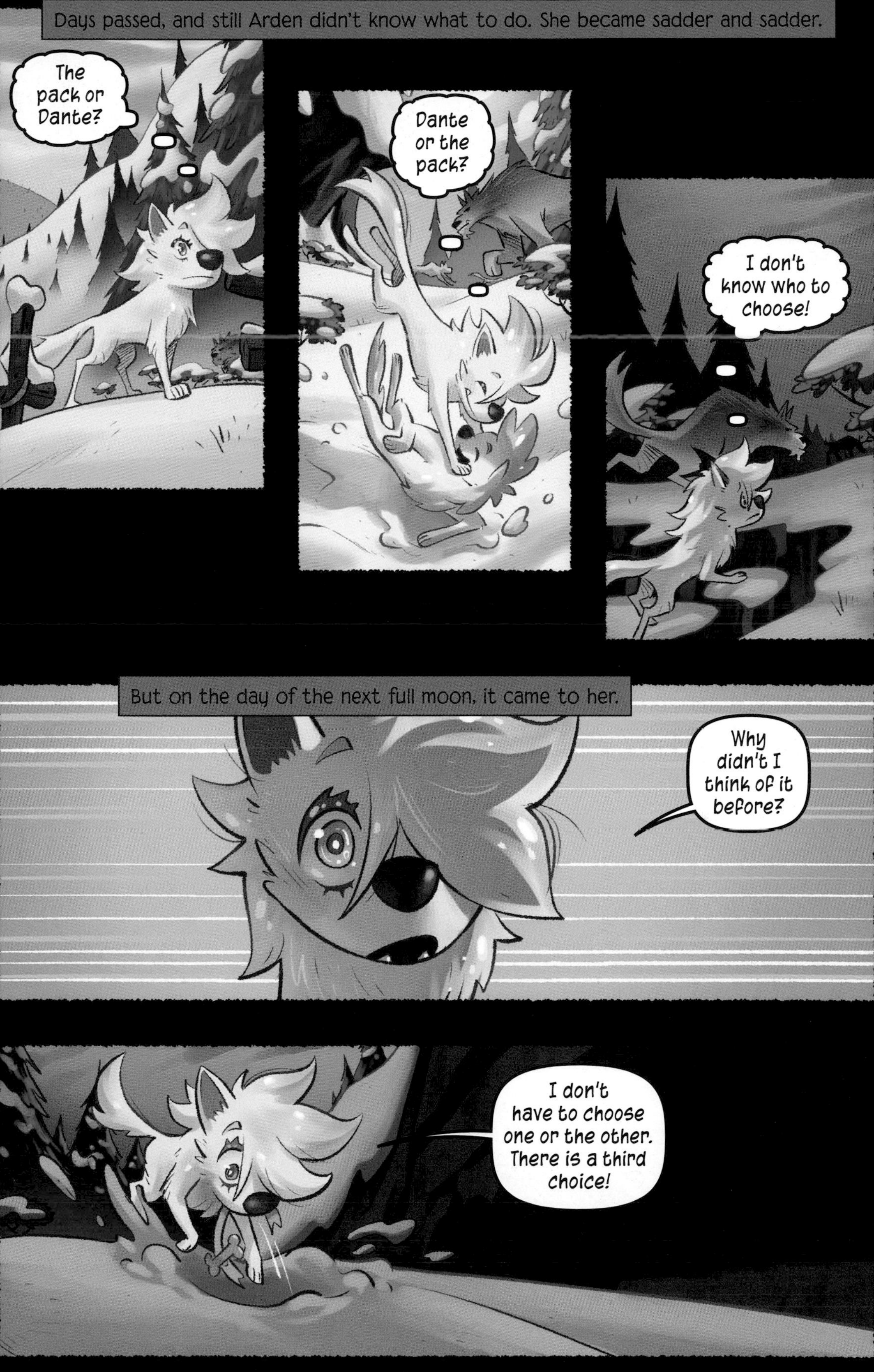

Days passed, and still Arden didn't know what to do. She became sadder and sadder.
The pack or Dante?
Dante or the pack?
I don't know who to choose!
But on the day of the next full moon, it came to her.
Why didn't I think of it before?
I don't have to choose one or the other. There is a third choice!

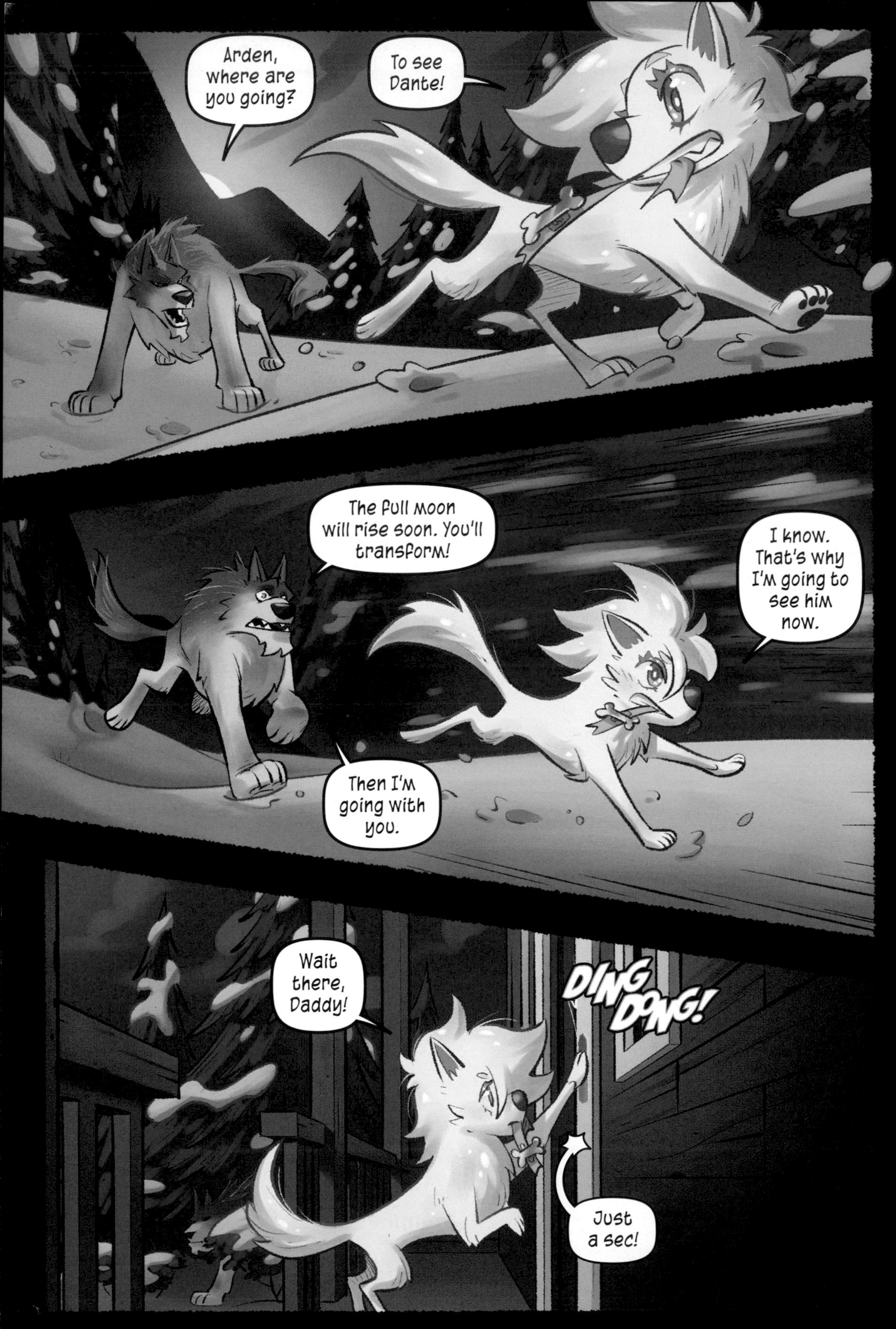
Arden, where are you going?
To see Dante!
The full moon will rise soon. You'll transform!
I know. That's why I'm going to see him now.
Then I'm going with you.
Wait there, Daddy!
DING DONG!
Just a sec!

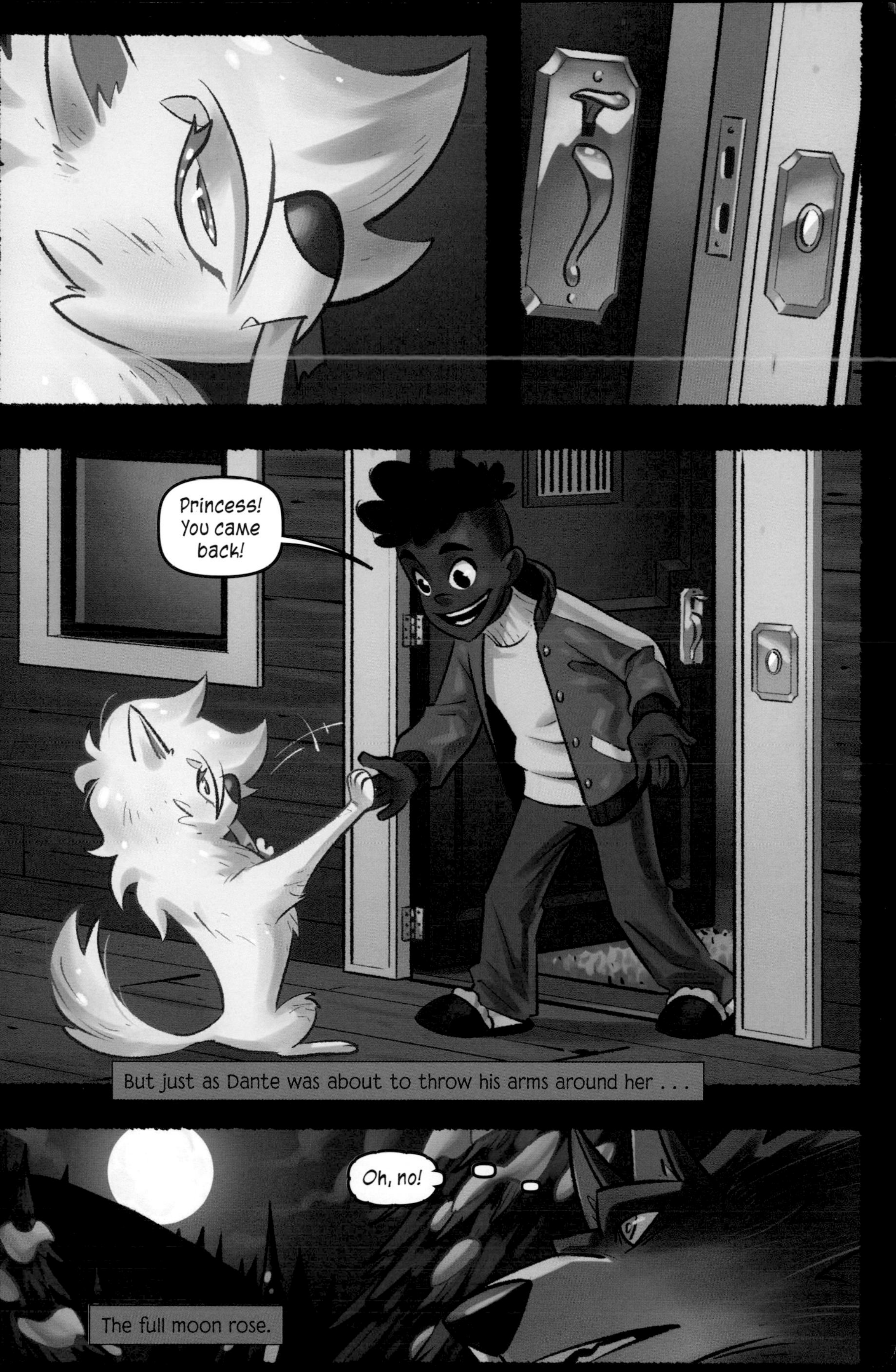

Princess! You came back!
But just as Dante was about to throw his arms around her . . .
Oh, no!
The full moon rose.

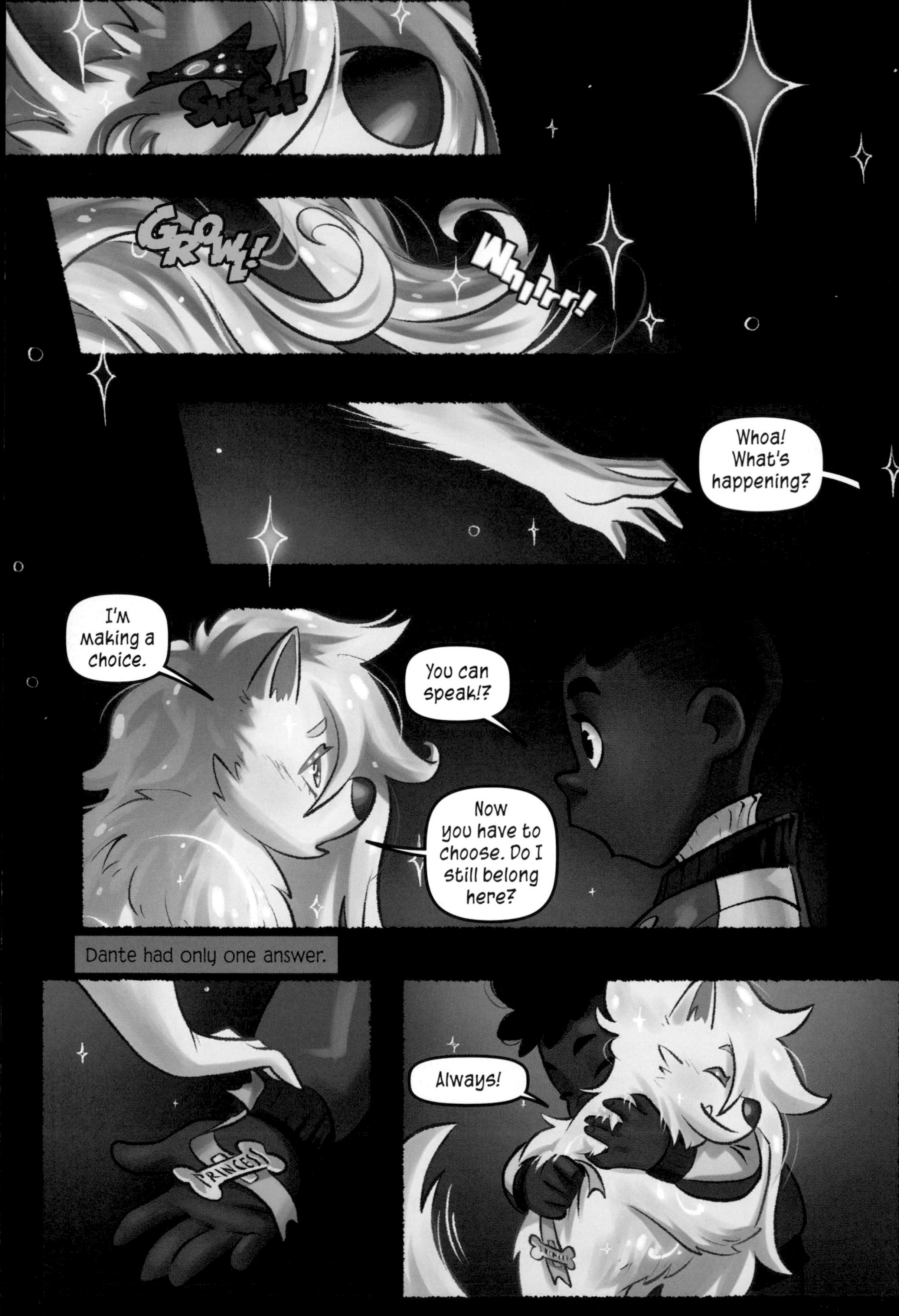
SWISH!
GROWL!
Whirrr!
Whoa! What's happening?
I'm making a choice.
You can speak!?
Now you have to choose. Do I still belong here?
Dante had only one answer.
PRINCESS
Always!

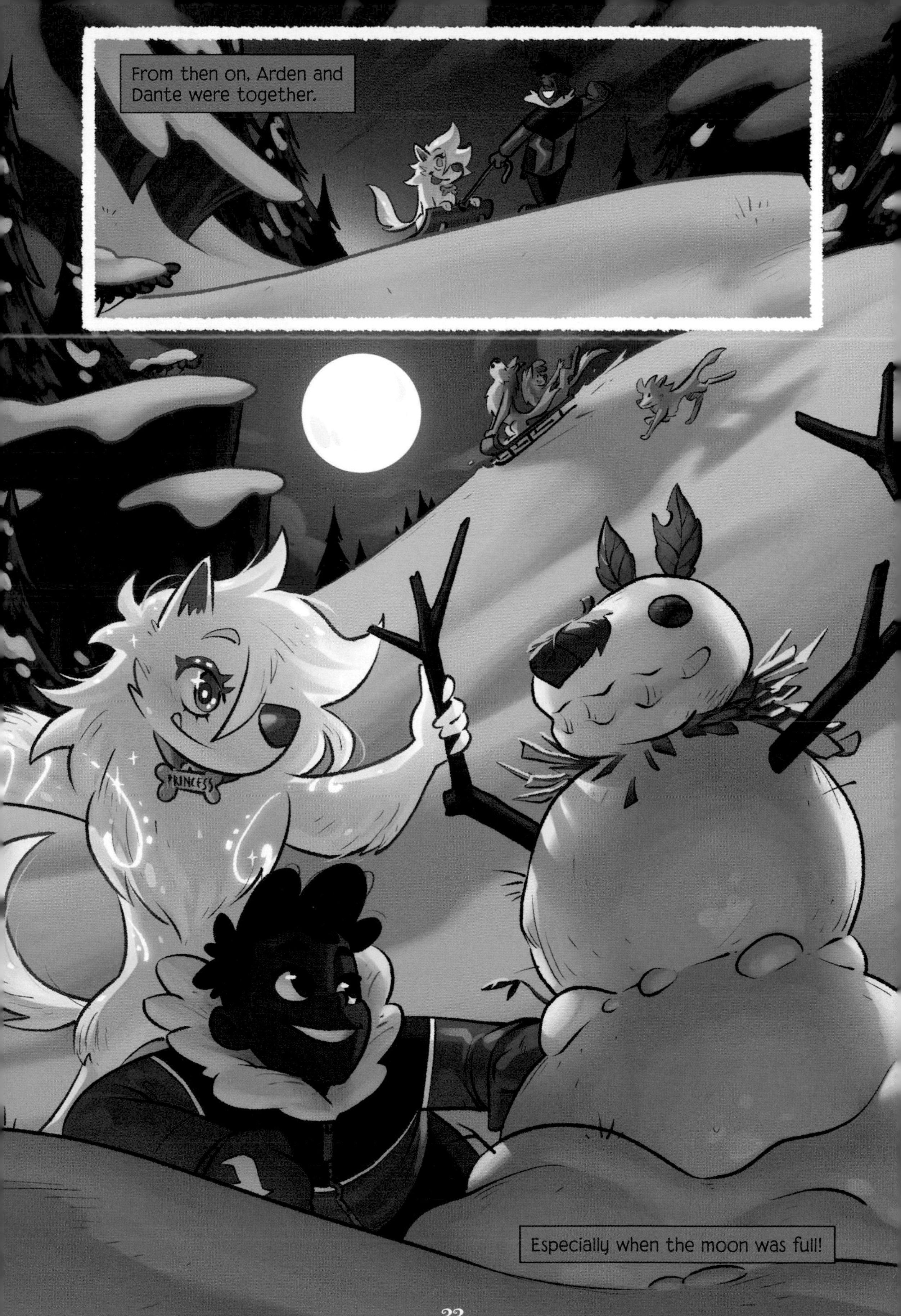
From then on, Arden and Dante were together.
PRINCESS
Especially when the moon was full!

ALL ABOUT THE ORIGINAL TALE!

The Little Mermaid, first published in April 1837, was written by Hans Christian Andersen of Denmark. In his story, the little mermaid falls in love with a handsome human prince she sees on a ship. When a terrible storm sinks the ship, she rescues the prince from drowning. She returns to her underwater kingdom, but she can't stop thinking about him. So she asks the sea witch for help. The sea witch gives her a potion that turns her mermaid tail into legs. In exchange, the witch takes the little mermaid's voice. And she gives the little mermaid a warning—if the prince doesn't return her love, the mermaid will dissolve into sea-foam.

The little mermaid hurries to the prince's kingdom. But to her despair, the prince marries a princess he believes saved him from the shipwreck! Heartbroken, the little mermaid is about to throw herself into the sea when her five sisters appear. They have a knife given to them by the sea witch in exchange for their long, beautiful hair. If the little mermaid kills the prince with the knife, she will change back into a mermaid. But the little mermaid chooses to sacrifice herself rather than hurt the prince. For her selfless act, she is transformed into a spirit of the air instead of sea-foam.

Andersen's classic tale has been retold in books, made into movies and television shows, and performed on stage. In some versions, the ending is much happier than the one in the original tale. Visitors to Copenhagen, Denmark, can see a famous bronze statue of the little mermaid sitting on a rock in the city's harbor.

A FAR OUT GUIDE TO THE FAIRYTALE'S TWISTS!

Instead of a little mermaid, the main character is a little werewolf.

The story takes place in the snowy mountains, not in an underwater kingdom

The little mermaid's potion gives her legs. Arden's potion will take away her curse

The little mermaid fell in love with a prince. Arden and Dante became best friends.

VISUAL QUESTIONS

Graphic novels use art to help tell a story. Arden finds several "treasures" on page 14. At the bottom of the page, she hears noises. Can you guess by the items she has found what the noises are?

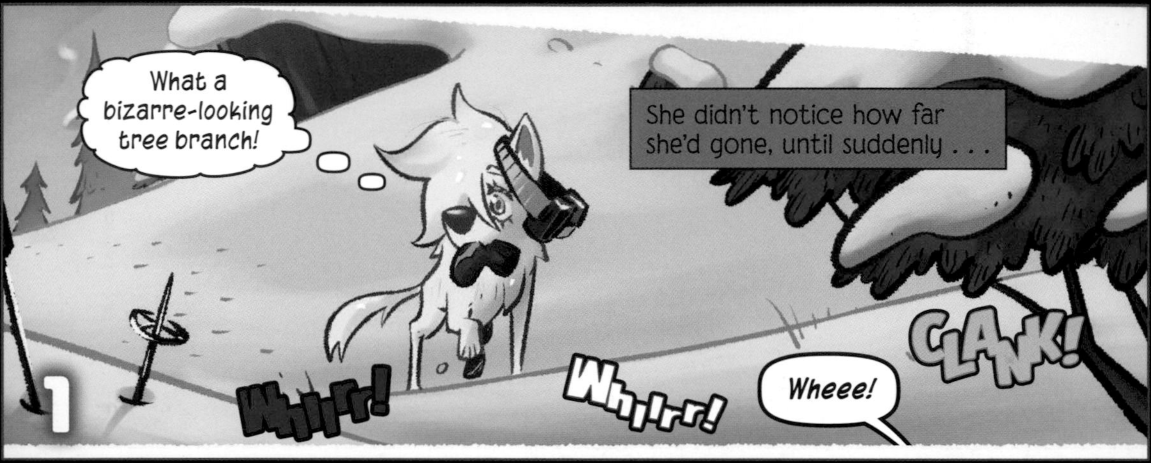
What a bizarre-looking tree branch!
She didn't notice how far she'd gone, until suddenly . . .
Whirrr!
Whirrr!
Wheee!
CLANK!
1

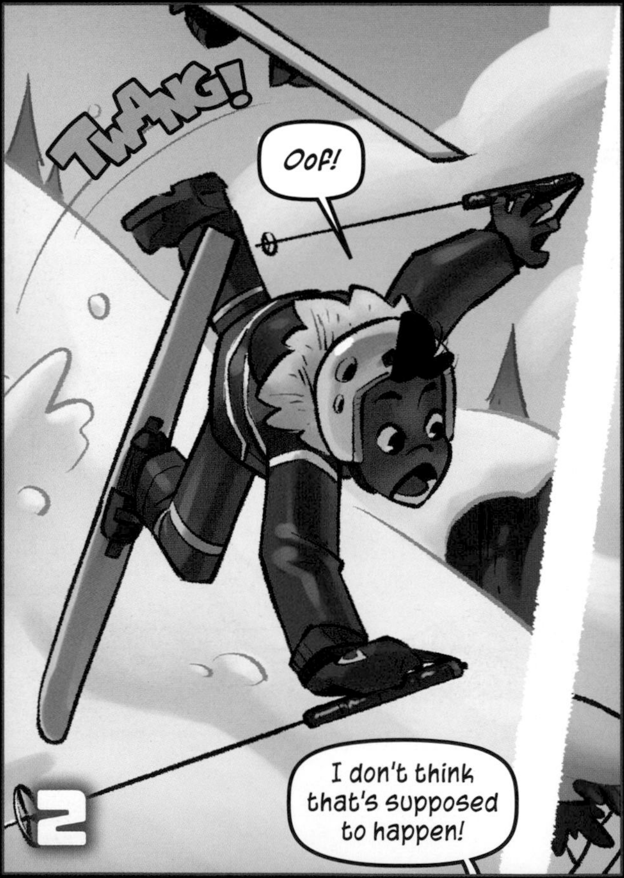
TWANG!
Oof!
I don't think that's supposed to happen!
2

A sound effect, or SFX for short, helps to show and describe sound in comics. What is making the SFX here? What other hints help explain the action?

Sometimes the art in graphic novels can hint at what is NOT seen. Who do you think is saying "Just a sec!" in this panel?

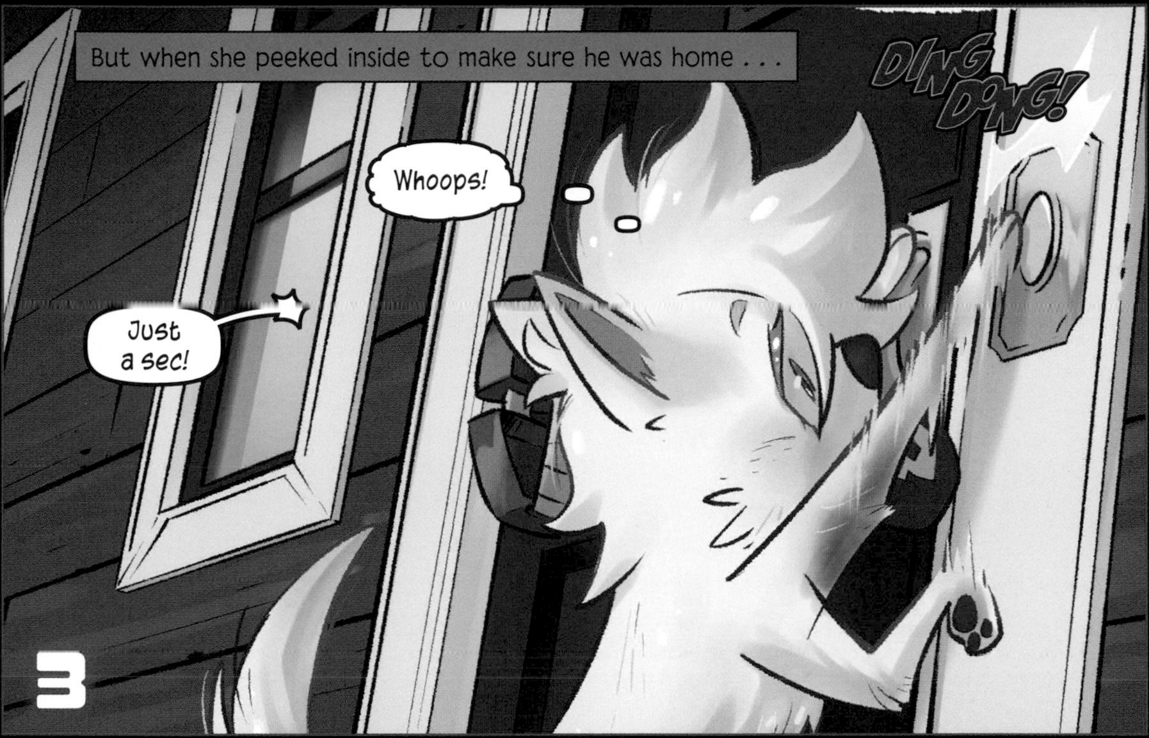
But when she peeked inside to make sure he was home . . .
DING DONG!
Whoops!
Just a sec!
3

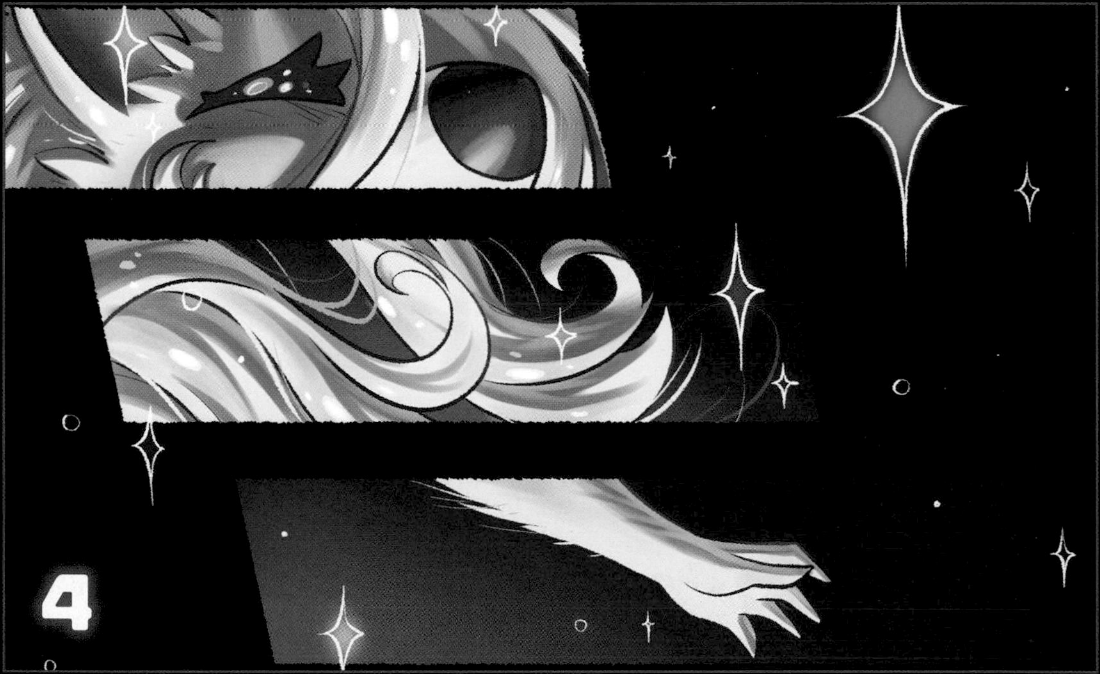
4

Sometimes the art in graphic novels breaks apart the action. What action do you think is happening here? Why do you think the artist broke it up?

AUTHOR

Stephanie True Peters has been writing books for young readers for more than 25 years. Among her most recent titles are *Sleeping Beauty: Magic Master* and *Johnny Slimeseed*, both for Capstone's Far-Out Fairy Tale/Folk Tale series. An avid reader, workout enthusiast, and beach wanderer, Stephanie enjoys spending time with her children, Jackson and Chloe, her husband, Dan, and the family's two cats and two rabbits. She lives and works in Mansfield, Massachusetts.

ILLUSTRATOR

Omar Lozano lives in Monterrey, Mexico. He has always loved illustration and is constantly on the lookout for amazing things to draw. In his free time, he watches lots of films, reads fantasy and sci-fi books, and draws! Omar has worked for Marvel Comics, DC Comics, IDW, Dark Horse Comics, Capstone, and several other publishing companies.

GLOSSARY

ancient (AYN-shunt)–from a long time ago

crone (KROHN)–a withered, witchlike old woman, or vulture in this instance

curse (KURSS)–an evil spell meant to harm someone

devastated (DEV-uh-stay-tid)–extremely upset and distressed

forbidden (for-BID-uhn)–not allowed, like ice cream for breakfast

mutt (MUHT)–a dog of mixed breed or unknown origin

pack (PAK)–a small group of animals that hunts together

potion (POH-shun)–a liquid or mixture of liquids thought to have magical effects

scamp (SKAMP)–a playful, mischievous, or naughty young person

transform (trans-FORM)–to change from one form to another